# Eclogues
### and
# Georgics

DOVER·THRIFT·EDITIONS

# Eclogues
## and
# Georgics

## VIRGIL

### Translated by James Rhoades

DOVER PUBLICATIONS, INC.
Mineola, New York

# DOVER THRIFT EDITIONS

GENERAL EDITOR: MARY CAROLYN WALDREP
EDITOR OF THIS VOLUME: SUSAN L. RATTINER

*Bibliographical Note*

This Dover edition, first published in 2005, is an unabridged republication of the James Rhoades translation of the *Eclogues and Georgics* by Virgil, as originally published by Oxford University Press, London and New York, in 1921 under the title *The Poems of Virgil*.

*Library of Congress Cataloging-in-Publication Data*

Virgil.
    [Bucolica. English]
    Eclogues and georgics / Virgil ; translated by James Rhoades.
        p. cm. — (Dover thrift editions)
    "An unabridged republication of the James Rhoades translation of the Eclogues and Georgics by Virgil, as originally published by Oxford University Press, London and New York, in 1921 under the title, The Poems of Virgil"—T.p. verso.
    ISBN 0-486-44559-3 (pbk.)
    1. Virgil—Translations into English. 2. Pastoral poetry, Latin—Translations into English. 3. Didactic poetry, Latin—Translations into English. 4. Country life—Poetry. 5. Agriculture—Poetry. I. Virgil. Georgica. English. 2005. II. Rhoades, James, 1841–1923. III. Title. IV. Series.

PA6807.B7 2005
873'.01—dc22

                                           2005045544

Manufactured in the United States of America
Dover Publications, Inc., 31 East 2nd Street, Mineola, N.Y. 11501

# Contents

# THE ECLOGUES

## Note

IN UNDERTAKING THUS, at the eleventh hour, to translate the Eclogues, I have availed myself of the published writings of the late Professor Conington, the late Mr. Arthur Sidgwick, and Professor J. W. Mackail, to whom my acknowledgements are due.

I have also, as the work proceeded, kept in touch with a free, but fine, unpublished version by him to whom my own is dedicated.

From this last, which was privately printed in 1899, among other verbal felicities, I was sorely tempted to borrow one perfect phrase, namely, "When winds had glassed the wave," for "cum placidum ventis staret mare" in Eclogue II. 26. And I now quote it here for the benefit of any whose eyes may light upon this page, because, taken in connexion with the context, it seems to me a flash of genius, and worthy to be accepted as the final rendering.

J. R.

KINGSTHORPE, KELVEDON, ESSEX,
*January* 1, 1921.

# ECLOGUE I

## MELIBOEUS. TITYRUS.

M.    You, Tityrus, 'neath a broad beech-canopy
    Reclining, on the slender oat rehearse
    Your silvan ditties: I from my sweet fields,
    And home's familiar bounds, even now depart.
    Exiled from home am I; while, Tityrus, you
    Sit careless in the shade, and, at your call,
    "Fair Amaryllis" bid the woods resound.

T.    O Meliboeus, 'twas a god vouchsafed
    This ease to us, for him a god will I
    Deem ever, and from my folds a tender lamb
    Oft with its life-blood shall his altar stain.
    His gift it is that, as your eyes may see,
    My kine may roam at large, and I myself
    Play on my shepherd's pipe what songs I will.

M.    I grudge you not the boon, but marvel more,
    Such wide confusion fills the country-side.
    See, sick at heart I drive my she-goats on,
    And this one, O my Tityrus, scarce can lead:
    For 'mid the hazel-thicket here but now
    She dropped her new-yeaned twins on the bare flint,
    Hope of the flock—an ill, I mind me well,
    Which many a time, but for my blinded sense,
    The thunder-stricken oak foretold, oft too
    From hollow trunk the raven's ominous cry.
    But who this god of yours? Come, Tityrus, tell.

T.    The city, Meliboeus, they call Rome,
    I, simpleton, deemed like this town of ours,
    Whereto we shepherds oft are wont to drive
    The younglings of the flock: so too I knew

Whelps to resemble dogs, and kids their dams,
Comparing small with great; but this as far
Above all other cities rears her head
As cypress above pliant osier towers.

M. And what so potent cause took you to Rome?

T. Freedom, which, though belated, cast at length
Her eyes upon the sluggard, when my beard
'Gan whiter fall beneath the barber's blade—
Cast eyes, I say, and, though long tarrying, came,
Now when, from Galatea's yoke released,
I serve but Amaryllis: for I will own,
While Galatea reigned over me, I had
No hope of freedom, and no thought to save.
Though many a victim from my folds went forth,
Or rich cheese pressed for the unthankful town,
Never with laden hands returned I home.

M. I used to wonder, Amaryllis, why
You cried to heaven so sadly, and for whom
You left the apples hanging on the trees;
'Twas Tityrus was away. Why, Tityrus,
The very pines, the very water-springs,
The very vineyards, cried aloud for you.

T. What could I do? how else from bonds be freed,
Or otherwhere find gods so nigh to aid?
There, Meliboeus, I saw that youth to whom
Yearly for twice six days my altars smoke.
There instant answer gave he to my suit,
"Feed, as before, your kine, boys, rear your bulls."

M. So in old age, you happy man, your fields
Will still be yours, and ample for your need!
Though, with bare stones o'erspread, the pastures all
Be choked with rushy mire, your ewes with young
By no strange fodder will be tried, nor hurt
Through taint contagious of a neighbouring flock.
Happy old man, who 'mid familiar streams
And hallowed springs, will court the cooling shade!
Here, as of old, your neighbour's bordering hedge,
That feasts with willow-flower the Hybla bees,
Shall oft with gentle murmur lull to sleep,
While the leaf-dresser beneath some tall rock
Uplifts his song, nor cease their cooings hoarse
The wood-pigeons that are your heart's delight,
Nor doves their moaning in the elm-tree top.

T.    Sooner shall light stags, therefore, feed in air,
       The seas their fish leave naked on the strand,
       Germans and Parthians shift their natural bounds,
       And these the Arar, those the Tigris drink,
       Than from my heart his face and memory fade.

M.    But we far hence, to burning Libya some,
       Some to the Scythian steppes, or thy swift flood,
       Cretan Oaxes, now must wend our way,
       Or Britain, from the whole world sundered far.
       Ah! shall I ever in aftertime behold
       My native bounds—see many a harvest hence
       With ravished eyes the lowly turf-roofed cot
       Where I was king? These fallows, trimmed so fair,
       Some brutal soldier will possess, these fields
       An alien master. Ah! to what a pass
       Has civil discord brought our hapless folk!
       For such as these, then, were our furrows sown!
       Now, Meliboeus, graft your pears, now set
       Your vines in order! Go, once happy flock,
       My she-goats, go. Never again shall I,
       Stretched in green cave, behold you from afar
       Hang from the bushy rock; my songs are sung;
       Never again will you, with me to tend,
       On clover-flower, or bitter willows, browse.

T.    Yet here, this night, you might repose with me,
       On green leaves pillowed: apples ripe have I,
       Soft chestnuts, and of curdled milk enow.
       And, see, the farm-roof chimneys smoke afar,
       And from the hills the shadows lengthening fall!

# ECLOGUE II

## ALEXIS.

The shepherd Corydon with love was fired
For fair Alexis, his own master's joy:
No room for hope had he, yet, none the less,
The thick-leaved shadowy-soaring beech-tree grove
Still would he haunt, and there alone, as thus,
To woods and hills pour forth his artless strains.
"Cruel Alexis, heed you naught my songs?
Have you no pity? you'll drive me to my death.
Now even the cattle court the cooling shade
And the green lizard hides him in the thorn:
Now for tired mowers, with the fierce heat spent,
Pounds Thestilis her mess of savoury herbs,
Wild thyme and garlic. I, with none beside,
Save hoarse cicalas shrilling through the brake,
Still track your footprints 'neath the broiling sun.
Better have borne the petulant proud disdain
Of Amaryllis, or Menalcas wooed,
Albeit he was so dark, and you so fair!
Trust not too much to colour, beauteous boy;
White privets fall, dark hyacinths are culled.
You scorn me, Alexis, who or what I am
Care not to ask—how rich in flocks, or how
In snow-white milk abounding: yet for me
Roam on Sicilian hills a thousand lambs;
Summer or winter, still my milk-pails brim.
I sing as erst Amphion of Circe sang,
What time he went to call his cattle home
On Attic Aracynthus. Nor am I
So ill to look on: lately on the beach

I saw myself, when winds had stilled the sea,
And, if that mirror lie not, would not fear
Daphnis to challenge, though yourself were judge.
Ah! were you but content with me to dwell.
Some lowly cot in the rough fields our home,
Shoot down the stags, or with green osier-wand
Round up the straggling flock! There you with me
In silvan strains will learn to rival Pan.
Pan first with wax taught reed with reed to join;
For sheep alike and shepherd Pan hath care.
Nor with the reed's edge fear you to make rough
Your dainty lip; such arts as these to learn
What did Amyntas do?—what did he not?
A pipe have I, of hemlock-stalks compact
In lessening lengths, Damoetas' dying-gift:
'Mine once,' quoth he, 'now yours, as heir to own.'
Foolish Amyntas heard and envied me.
Ay, and two fawns, I risked my neck to find
In a steep glen, with coats white-dappled still,
From a sheep's udders suckled twice a day—
These still I keep for you; which Thestilis
Implores me oft to let her lead away;
And she shall have them, since my gifts you spurn.
Come hither, beauteous boy; for you the Nymphs
Bring baskets, see, with lilies brimmed; for you,
Plucking pale violets and poppy-heads,
Now the fair Naiad, of narcissus flower
And fragrant fennel, doth one posy twine—
With cassia then, and other scented herbs,
Blends them, and sets the tender hyacinth off
With yellow marigold. I too will pick
Quinces all silvered-o'er with hoary down,
Chestnuts, which Amaryllis wont to love,
And waxen plums withal: this fruit no less
Shall have its meed of honour; and I will pluck
You too, ye laurels, and you, ye myrtles, near,
For so your sweets ye mingle. Corydon,
You are a boor, nor heeds a whit your gifts
Alexis; no, nor would Iollas yield,
Should gifts decide the day. Alack! alack!
What misery have I brought upon my head!—
Loosed on the flowers Siroces to my bane,
And the wild boar upon my crystal springs!

Whom do you fly, infatuate? gods ere now,
And Dardan Paris, have made the woods their home.
Let Pallas keep the towers her hand hath built,
Us before all things let the woods delight.
The grim-eyed lioness pursues the wolf,
The wolf the she-goat, the she-goat herself
In wanton sport the flowering cytisus,
And Corydon Alexis, each led on
By their own longing. See, the ox comes home
With plough up-tilted, and the shadows grow
To twice their length with the departing sun,
Yet me love burns, for who can limit love?
Ah! Corydon, Corydon, what hath crazed your wit?
Your vine half-pruned hangs on the leafy elm;
Why haste you not to weave what need requires
Of pliant rush or osier? Scorned by this,
Elsewhere some new Alexis you will find."

# ECLOGUE III

### MENALCAS. DAMOETAS. PALAEMON.

M.   Who owns the flock, Damoetas? Meliboeus?
D.   Nay, they are Aegon's sheep, of late by him
      Committed to my care.
M.                       O every way
      Unhappy sheep, unhappy flock! while he
      Still courts Neaera, fearing lest her choice
      Should fall on me, this hireling shepherd here
      Wrings hourly twice their udders, from the flock
      Filching the life-juice, from the lambs their milk.
D.   Hold! not so ready with your jeers at men!
      We know who once, and in what shrine with you—
      The he-goats looked aside—the light nymphs laughed—
M.   Ay, then, I warrant, when they saw *me* slash
      Micon's young vines and trees with spiteful hook.
D.   Or here by these old beeches, when you broke
      The bow and arrows of Damon; for you chafed
      When first you saw them given to the boy,
      Cross-grained Menalcas, ay, and had you not
      Done him some mischief, would have chafed to death.
M.   With thieves so daring, what can masters do?
      Did I not see you, rogue, in ambush lie
      For Damon's goat, while loud Lycisca barked?
      And when I cried, "Where is he off to now?
      Gather your flock together, Tityrus,"
      You hid behind the sedges.
D.                    Well, was he
      Whom I had conquered still to keep the goat.
      Which in the piping-match my pipe had won!
      You may not know it, but the goat was mine.

M.   *You* out-pipe *him?* when had you ever pipe
      Wax-welded? in the cross-ways used you not
      On grating straw some miserable tune
      To mangle?

D.            Well, then, shall we try our skill
      Each against each in turn? Lest you be loth,
      I pledge this heifer; every day she comes
      Twice to the milking-pail, and feeds withal
      Two young ones at her udder: say you now
      What you will stake upon the match with me.

M.   Naught from the flock I'll venture, for at home
      I have a father and a step-dame harsh,
      And twice a day both reckon up the flock,
      And one withal the kids. But I will stake,
      Seeing you are so mad, what you yourself
      Will own more priceless far—two beechen cups
      By the divine art of Alcimedon
      Wrought and embossed, whereon a limber vine,
      Wreathed round them by the graver's facile tool,
      Twines over clustering ivy-berries pale.
      Two figures, one Conon, in the midst he set,
      And one—how call you him, who with his wand
      Marked out for all men the whole round of heaven,
      That they who reap, or stoop behind the plough,
      Might know their several seasons? Nor as yet
      Have I set lip to them, but lay them by.

D.   For me too wrought the same Alcimedon
      A pair of cups, and round the handles wreathed
      Pliant acanthus, Orpheus in the midst,
      The forests following in his wake; nor yet
      Have I set lip to them, but lay them by.
      Matched with a heifer, who would prate of cups?

M.   You shall not balk me now; where'er you bid,
      I shall be with you; only let us have
      For auditor—or see, to serve our turn,
      Yonder Palaemon comes! In singing-bouts
      I'll see you play the challenger no more.

D.   Out then with what you have; I shall not shrink,
      Nor budge for any man: only do you,
      Neighbour Palaemon, with your whole heart's skill—
      For it is no slight matter—play your part.

P.   Say on then, since on the green sward we sit,
      And now is burgeoning both field and tree;

Now is the forest green, and now the year
At fairest. Do you first, Damoetas, sing,
Then you, Menalcas, in alternate strain:
Alternate strains are to the Muses dear.

D.    "From Jove the Muse began; Jove filleth all,
Makes the earth fruitful, for my songs hath care."

M.    "Me Phoebus loves; for Phoebus his own gifts,
Bays and sweet-blushing hyacinths, I keep."

D.    "Gay Galatea throws an apple at me,
Then hies to the willows, hoping to be seen."

M.    "My dear Amyntas comes unasked to me;
Not Delia to my dogs is better known."

D.    "Gifts for my love I've found; mine eyes have marked
Where the wood-pigeons build their airy nests."

M.    "Ten golden apples have I sent my boy,
All that I could, to-morrow as many more."

D.    "What words to me, and uttered O how oft,
Hath Galatea spoke! waft some of them,
Ye winds, I pray you, for the gods to hear."

M.    "It profiteth me naught, Amyntas mine,
That in your very heart you spurn me not,
If, while you hunt the boar, I guard the nets."

D.    "Prithee, Iollas, for my birthday guest
Send me your Phyllis; when for the young crops
I slay my heifer, you yourself shall come."

M.    "I am all hers; she wept to see me go,
And, lingering on the word, 'farewell' she said,
'My beautiful Iollas, fare you well.'"

D.    "Fell as the wolf is to the folded flock,
Rain to ripe corn, Sirocco to the trees,
The wrath of Amaryllis is to me."

M.    "As moisture to the corn, to ewes with young
Lithe willow, as arbute to the yeanling kids,
So sweet Amyntas, and none else, to me."

D.    "My Muse, although she be but country-bred,
Is loved by Pollio: O Pierian Maids,
Pray you, a heifer for your reader feed!"

M.    "Pollio himself too doth new verses make:
Feed ye a bull now ripe to butt with horn,
And scatter with his hooves the flying sand."

D.    "Who loves thee, Pollio, may he thither come
Where thee he joys beholding; ay, for him
Let honey flow, the thorn-bush spices bear."

M.    "Who hates not Bavius, let him also love
      Thy songs, O Maevius, ay, and therewithal
      Yoke foxes to his car, and he-goats milk."

D.    "You, picking flowers and strawberries that grow
      So near the ground, fly hence, boys, get you gone!
      There's a cold adder lurking in the grass."

M.    "Forbear, my sheep, to tread too near the brink;
      Yon bank is ill to trust to; even now
      The ram himself, see, dries his dripping fleece!"

D.    "Back with the she-goats, Tityrus, grazing there
      So near the river! I, when time shall serve,
      Will take them all, and wash them in the pool."

M.    "Boys, get your sheep together; if the heat,
      As late it did, forestall us with the milk,
      Vainly the dried-up udders shall we wring."

D.    "How lean my bull amid the fattening vetch!
      Alack! alack! for herdsman and for herd!
      It is the self-same love that wastes us both."

M.    "These truly—nor is even love the cause—
      Scarce have the flesh to keep their bones together
      Some evil eye my lambkins hath bewitched."

D.    "Say in what clime—and you shall be withal
      My great Apollo—the whole breadth of heaven
      Opens no wider than three ells to view."

M.    "Say in what country grow such flowers as bear
      The names of kings upon their petals writ,
      And you shall have fair Phyllis for your own."

P.    Not mine betwixt such rivals to decide:
      You well deserve the heifer, so does he,
      With all who either fear the sweets of love,
      Or taste its bitterness. Now, boys, shut off
      The sluices, for the fields have drunk their fill.

# ECLOGUE IV

## POLLIO.

Muses of Sicily, essay we now
A somewhat loftier task! Not all men love
Coppice or lowly tamarisk: sing we woods,
Woods worthy of a Consul let them be.
   Now the last age by Cumae's Sibyl sung
Has come and gone, and the majestic roll
Of circling centuries begins anew:
Justice returns, returns old Saturn's reign,
With a new breed of men sent down from heaven.
Only do thou, at the boy's birth in whom
The iron shall cease, the golden race arise,
Befriend him, chaste Lucina; 'tis thine own
Apollo reigns. And in thy consulate,
This glorious age, O Pollio, shall begin,
And the months enter on their mighty march.
Under thy guidance, whatso tracks remain
Of our old wickedness, once done away,
Shall free the earth from never-ceasing fear.
He shall receive the life of gods, and see
Heroes with gods commingling, and himself
Be seen of them, and with his father's worth
Reign o'er a world at peace. For thee, O boy,
First shall the earth, untilled, pour freely forth
Her childish gifts, the gadding ivy-spray
With foxglove and Egyptian bean-flower mixed,
And laughing-eyed acanthus. Of themselves,
Untended, will the she-goats then bring home
Their udders swollen with milk, while flocks afield
Shall of the monstrous lion have no fear.

11

Thy very cradle shall pour forth for thee
Caressing flowers. The serpent too shall die,
Die shall the treacherous poison-plant, and far
And wide Assyrian spices spring. But soon
As thou hast skill to read of heroes' fame,
And of thy father's deeds, and inly learn
What virtue is, the plain by slow degrees
With waving corn-crops shall to golden grow,
From the wild briar shall hang the blushing grape,
And stubborn oaks sweat honey-dew. Nathless
Yet shall there lurk within of ancient wrong
Some traces, bidding tempt the deep with ships,
Gird towns with walls, with furrows cleave the earth.
Therewith a second Tiphys shall there be,
Her hero-freight a second Argo bear;
New wars too shall arise, and once again
Some great Achilles to some Troy be sent.
Then, when the mellowing years have made thee man,
No more shall mariner sail, nor pine-tree bark
Ply traffic on the sea, but every land
Shall all things bear alike: the glebe no more
Shall feel the harrow's grip, nor vine the hook;
The sturdy ploughman shall loose yoke from steer,
Nor wool with varying colours learn to lie;
But in the meadows shall the ram himself,
Now with soft flush of purple, now with tint
Of yellow saffron, teach his fleece to shine.
While clothed in natural scarlet graze the lambs.
"Such still, such ages weave ye, as ye run,"
Sang to their spindles the consenting Fates
By Destiny's unalterable decree.
Assume thy greatness, for the time draws nigh,
Dear child of gods, great progeny of Jove!
See how it totters—the world's orbèd might,
Earth, and wide ocean, and the vault profound,
All, see, enraptured of the coming time!
Ah! might such length of days to me be given,
And breath suffice me to rehearse thy deeds,
Nor Thracian Orpheus should out-sing me then,
Nor Linus, though his mother this, and that
His sire should aid—Orpheus Calliope,
And Linus fair Apollo. Nay, though Pan,
With Arcady for judge, my claim contest,

With Arcady for judge great Pan himself
Should own him foiled, and from the field retire.
  Begin to greet thy mother with a smile,
O baby-boy! ten months of weariness
For thee she bore: O baby-boy, begin!
For him, on whom his parents have not smiled,
Gods deem not worthy of their board or bed.

# ECLOGUE V

### MENALCAS. MOPSUS.

ME.   Why, Mopsus, being both together met,
      You skilled to breathe upon the slender reeds,
      I to sing ditties, do we not sit down
      Here where the elm-trees and the hazels blend?

MO.   You are the elder, 'tis for me to bide
      Your choice, Menalcas, whether now we seek
      Yon shade that quivers to the changeful breeze,
      Or the cave's shelter. Look you how the cave
      Is with the wild vine's clusters over-laced!

ME.   None but Amyntas on these hills of ours
      Can vie with you.

MO.               What if he also strive
      To out-sing Phoebus?

ME.                Do you first begin,
      Good Mopsus, whether minded to sing aught
      Of Phyllis and her loves, or Alcon's praise,
      Or to fling taunts at Codrus. Come, begin,
      While Tityrus watches o'er the grazing kids.

MO.   Nay, then, I will essay what late I carved
      On a green beech-tree's rind, playing by turns,
      And marking down the notes; then afterward
      Bid you Amyntas match them if he can.

ME.   As limber willow to pale olive yields,
      As lowly Celtic nard to rose-buds bright,
      So, to my mind, Amyntas yields to you.
      But hold awhile, for to the cave we come.

MO.   "For Daphnis cruelly slain wept all the Nymphs—
      Ye hazels, bear them witness, and ye streams—
      When she, his mother, clasping in her arms
      The hapless body of the son she bare,

14

To gods and stars unpitying poured her plaint.
Then, Daphnis, to the cooling streams were none
That drove the pastured oxen, then no beast
Drank of the river, or would the grass-blade touch.
Nay, the wild rocks and woods then voiced the roar
Of Afric lions mourning for thy death.
Daphnis, 'twas thou bad'st yoke to Bacchus' car
Armenian tigresses, lead on the pomp
Of revellers, and with tender foliage wreathe
The bending spear-wands. As to trees the vine
Is crown of glory, as to vines the grape,
Bulls to the herd, to fruitful fields the corn,
So the one glory of thine own art thou.
When the Fates took thee hence, then Pales' self,
And even Apollo, left the country lone.
Where the plump barley-grain so oft we sowed,
There but wild oats and barren darnel spring;
For tender violet and narcissus bright
Thistle and prickly thorn uprear their heads.
Now, O ye shepherds, strew the ground with leaves,
And o'er the fountains draw a shady veil—
So Daphnis to his memory bids be done—
And rear a tomb, and write thereon this verse:
'I, Daphnis in the woods, from hence in fame
Am to the stars exalted, guardian once
Of a fair flock, myself more fair than they.'"

ME.  So is thy song to me, poet divine,
As slumber on the grass to weary limbs,
Or to slake thirst from some sweet-bubbling rill
In summer's heat. Nor on the reeds alone,
But with thy voice art thou, thrice happy boy,
Ranked with thy master, second but to him.
Yet will I, too, in turn, as best I may,
Sing thee a song, and to the stars uplift
Thy Daphnis—Daphnis to the stars extol,
For me too Daphnis loved.

MO.              Than such a boon
What dearer could I deem? the boy himself
Was worthy to be sung, and many a time
Hath Stimichon to me your singing praised.

ME.  "In dazzling sheen with unaccustomed eyes
Daphnis stands rapt before Olympus' gate,
And sees beneath his feet the clouds and stars.

Wherefore the woods and fields, Pan, shepherd-folk,
And Dryad-maidens, thrill with eager joy;
Nor wolf with treacherous wile assails the flock,
Nor nets the stag: kind Daphnis loveth peace.
The unshorn mountains to the stars up-toss
Voices of gladness; ay, the very rocks,
The very thickets, shout and sing, 'A god,
A god is he, Menalcas!' Be thou kind,
Propitious to thine own. Lo! altars four,
Twain to thee, Daphnis, and to Phoebus twain
For sacrifice, we build; and I for thee
Two beakers yearly of fresh milk a-foam,
And of rich olive-oil two bowls, will set;
And of the wine-god's bounty above all,
If cold, before the hearth, or in the shade
At harvest-time, to glad the festal hour,
From flasks of Ariusian grape will pour
Sweet nectar. Therewithal at my behest
Shall Lyctian Aegon and Damoetas sing,
And Alphesiboeus emulate in dance
The dancing Satyrs. This, thy service due,
Shalt thou lack never, both when we pay the Nymphs
Our yearly vows, and when with lustral rites
The fields we hallow. Long as the wild boar
Shall love the mountain-heights, and fish the streams,
While bees on thyme and crickets feed on dew,
Thy name, thy praise, thine honour, shall endure.
Even as to Bacchus and to Ceres, so
To thee the swain his yearly vows shall make;
And thou thereof, like them, shalt quittance claim."

Mo.   How, how repay thee for a song so rare?
For not the whispering south-wind on its way
So much delights me, nor wave-smitten beach,
Nor streams that race adown their bouldered beds.

Me.   First this frail hemlock-stalk to you I give,
Which taught me "Corydon with love was fired
For fair Alexis," ay, and this beside,
"Who owns the flock?—Meliboeus?"

Mo.                   But take you
This shepherd's crook, which, howso hard he begged,
Antigenes, then worthy to be loved,
Prevailed not to obtain—with brass, you see,
And equal knots, Menalcas, fashioned fair!

# ECLOGUE VI

## To Varus.

First my Thalia stooped in sportive mood
To Syracusan strains, nor blushed within
The woods to house her. When I sought to tell
Of battles and of kings, the Cynthian god
Plucked at mine ear and warned me: "Tityrus,
Beseems a shepherd-wight to feed fat sheep,
But sing a slender song." Now, Varus, I—
For lack there will not who would laud thy deeds,
And treat of dolorous wars—will rather tune
To the slim oaten reed my silvan lay.
I sing but as vouchsafed me; yet even this
If, if but one with ravished eyes should read,
Of thee, O Varus, shall our tamarisks
And all the woodland ring; nor can there be
A page more dear to Phoebus, than the page
Where, foremost writ, the name of Varus stands.
  Speed ye, Pierian Maids! Within a cave
Young Chromis and Mnasyllos chanced to see
Silenus sleeping, flushed, as was his wont,
With wine of yesterday. Not far aloof,
Slipped from his head, the garlands lay, and there
By its worn handle hung a ponderous cup.
Approaching—for the old man many a time
Had balked them both of a long hoped-for song—
Garlands to fetters turned, they bind him fast.
Then Aeglë, fairest of the Naiad-band,
Aeglë came up to the half-frightened boys,
Came, and, as now with open eyes he lay,
With juice of blood-red mulberries smeared him o'er,
Both brow and temples. Laughing at their guile,

And crying, "Why tie the fetters? loose me, boys;
Enough for you to think you had the power;
Now list the songs you wish for—songs for you,
Another meed for her"—forthwith began.
Then might you see the wild things of the wood,
With Fauns in sportive frolic beat the time,
And stubborn oaks their branchy summits bow.
Not Phoebus doth the rude Parnassian crag
So ravish, nor Orpheus so entrance the heights
Of Rhodope or Ismarus: for he sang
How through the mighty void the seeds were driven
Of earth, air, ocean, and of liquid fire,
How all that is from these beginnings grew,
And the young world itself took solid shape,
Then 'gan its crust to harden, and in the deep
Shut Nereus off, and mould the forms of things
Little by little; and how the earth amazed
Beheld the new sun shining, and the showers
Fall, as the clouds soared higher, what time the woods
'Gan first to rise, and living things to roam
Scattered among the hills that knew them not.
Then sang he of the stones by Pyrrha cast,
Of Saturn's reign, and of Prometheus' theft,
And the Caucasian birds, and told withal
Nigh to what fountain by his comrades left
The mariners cried on Hylas, till the shore
Re-echoed "Hylas, Hylas!" Then he soothed
Pasiphaë with the love of her white bull—
Happy if cattle-kind had never been!—
O ill-starred maid, what frenzy caught thy soul
The daughters too of Proetus filled the fields
With their feigned lowings, yet no one of them
Of such unhallowed union e'er was fain
As with a beast to mate, though many a time
On her smooth forehead she had sought for horns,
And for her neck had feared the galling plough.
O ill-starred maid! thou roamest now the hills,
While on soft hyacinths he, his snowy side
Reposing, under some dark ilex now
Chews the pale herbage, or some heifer tracks
Amid the crowding herd. Now close, ye Nymphs,
Ye Nymphs of Dicte, close the forest-glades,
If haply there may chance upon mine eyes

The white bull's wandering foot-prints: him belike
Following the herd, or by green pasture lured,
Some kine may guide to the Gortynian stalls.
Then sings he of the maid so wonder-struck
With the apples of the Hesperids, and then
With moss-bound, bitter bark rings round the forms
Of Phaëthon's fair sisters, from the ground
Up-towering into poplars. Next he sings
Of Gallus wandering by Permessus' stream,
And by a sister of the Muses led
To the Aonian mountains, and how all
The choir of Phoebus rose to greet him; how
The shepherd Linus, singer of songs divine,
Brow-bound with flowers and bitter parsley, spake:
"These reeds the Muses give thee, take them thou,
Erst to the agèd bard of Ascra given,
Wherewith in singing he was wont to draw
Time-rooted ash-trees from the mountain heights.
With these the birth of the Grynean grove
Be voiced by thee, that of no grove beside
Apollo more may boast him." Wherefore speak
Of Scylla, child of Nisus, who, 'tis said,
Her fair white loins with barking monsters girt
Vexed the Dulichian ships, and, in the deep
Swift-eddying whirlpool, with her sea-dogs tore
The trembling mariners? or how he told
Of the changed limbs of Tereus—what a feast,
What gifts, to him by Philomel were given;
How swift she sought the desert, with what wings
Hovered in anguish o'er her ancient home?
All that, of old, Eurotas, happy stream,
Heard, as Apollo mused upon the lyre,
And bade his laurels learn, Silenus sang;
Till from Olympus, loth at his approach,
Vesper, advancing, bade the shepherds tell
Their tale of sheep, and pen them in the fold.

# ECLOGUE VII

### MELIBOEUS. CORYDON. THYRSIS.

Daphnis beneath a rustling ilex-tree
Had sat him down; Thyrsis and Corydon
Had gathered in the flock, Thyrsis the sheep,
And Corydon the she-goats swollen with milk—
Both in the flower of age, Arcadians both,
Ready to sing, and in like strain reply.
Hither had strayed, while from the frost I fend
My tender myrtles, the he-goat himself,
Lord of the flock; when Daphnis I espy!
Soon as he saw me, "Hither haste," he cried,
"O Meliboeus! goat and kids are safe;
And, if you have an idle hour to spare,
Rest here beneath the shade. Hither the steers
Will through the meadows, of their own free will,
Untended come to drink. Here Mincius hath
With tender rushes rimmed his verdant banks,
And from yon sacred oak with busy hum
The bees are swarming." What was I to do?
No Phyllis or Alcippe left at home
Had I, to shelter my new-weanèd lambs,
And no slight matter was a singing-bout
'Twixt Corydon and Thyrsis. Howsoe'er,
I let my business wait upon their sport.
So they began to sing, voice answering voice
In strains alternate—for alternate strains
The Muses then were minded to recall—
First Corydon, then Thyrsis in reply.

C.   "Libethrian Nymphs, who are my heart's delight,
Grant me, as doth my Codrus, so to sing—
Next to Apollo he—or if to this

We may not all attain, my tuneful pipe
Here on this sacred pine shall silent hang."

T.  "Arcadian shepherds, wreathe with ivy-spray
Your budding poet, so that Codrus burst
With envy: if he praise beyond my due,
Then bind my brow with foxglove, lest his tongue
With evil omen blight the coming bard."

C.  "This bristling boar's head, Delian Maid, to thee,
With branching antlers of a sprightly stag,
Young Micon offers: if his luck but hold,
Full-length in polished marble, ankle-bound
With purple buskin, shall thy statue stand."

T.  "A bowl of milk, Priapus, and these cakes,
Yearly, it is enough for thee to claim;
Thou art the guardian of a poor man's plot.
Wrought for a while in marble, if the flock
At lambing time be filled, stand there in gold."

C.  "Daughter of Nereus, Galatea mine,
Sweeter than Hybla-thyme, more white than swans,
Fairer than ivy pale, soon as the steers
Shall from their pasture to the stalls repair,
If aught for Corydon thou carest, come."

T.  "Now may I seem more bitter to your taste
Than herb Sardinian, rougher than the broom,
More worthless than strewn sea-weed, if to-day
Hath not a year out-lasted! Fie for shame!
Go home, my cattle, from your grazing go!"

C.  "Ye mossy springs, and grass more soft than sleep,
And arbute green with thin shade sheltering you,
Ward off the solstice from my flock, for now
Comes on the burning summer, now the buds
Upon the limber vine-shoot 'gin to swell."

T.  "Here is a hearth, and resinous logs, here fire
Unstinted, and doors black with ceaseless smoke.
Here heed we Boreas' icy breath as much
As the wolf heeds the number of the flock,
Or furious rivers their restraining banks."

C.  "The junipers and prickly chestnuts stand,
And 'neath each tree lie strewn their several fruits,
Now the whole world is smiling, but if fair
Alexis from these hill-slopes should away,
Even the rivers you would see run dry."

T.  "The field is parched, the grass-blades thirst to death

In the faint air; Liber hath grudged the hills
His vine's o'er-shadowing: should my Phyllis come,
Green will be all the grove, and Jupiter
Descend in floods of fertilizing rain."

C. "The poplar doth Alcides hold most dear,
The vine Iacchus, Phoebus his own bays,
And Venus fair the myrtle: therewithal
Phyllis doth hazels love, and while she loves,
Myrtle nor bay the hazel shall out-vie."

T. "Ash in the forest is most beautiful,
Pine in the garden, poplar by the stream,
Fir on the mountain-height; but if more oft
Thou'ldst come to me, fair Lycidas, to thee
Both forest-ash, and garden-pine should bow."

M. These I remember, and how Thyrsis strove
For victory in vain. From that time forth
Is Corydon still Corydon with us.

# ECLOGUE VIII

## To Pollio.
### Damon. Alphesiboeus.

Of Damon and Alphesiboeus now,
Those shepherd-singers at whose rival strains
The heifer wondering forgot to graze,
The lynx stood awe-struck, and the flowing streams,
Unwonted loiterers, stayed their course to hear—
How Damon and Alphesiboeus sang
Their pastoral ditties, will I tell the tale.
 Thou, whether broad Timavus' rocky banks
Thou now art passing, or dost skirt the shore
Of the Illyrian main,—will ever dawn
That day when I thy deeds may celebrate,
Ever that day when through the whole wide world
I may renown thy verse—that verse alone
Of Sophoclean buskin worthy found?
With thee began, to thee shall end, the strain.
Take thou these songs that owe their birth to thee,
And deign around thy temples to let creep
This ivy-chaplet 'twixt the conquering bays.
 Scarce had night's chilly shade forsook the sky
What time to nibbling sheep the dewy grass
Tastes sweetest, when, on his smooth shepherd-staff
Of olive leaning, Damon thus began.

D. "Rise, Lucifer, and, heralding the light,
Bring in the genial day, while I make moan
Fooled by vain passion for a faithless bride,
For Nysa, and with this my dying breath
Call on the gods, though little it bestead—
The gods who heard her vows and heeded not.

23

"Begin, my flute, with me Maenalian lays.
Ever hath Maenalus his murmuring groves
And whispering pines, and ever hears the songs
Of love-lorn shepherds, and of Pan, who first
Brooked not the tuneful reed should idle lie.

"Begin, my flute, with me Maenalian lays.
Nysa to Mopsus given! what may not then
We lovers look for? soon shall we see mate
Griffins with mares, and in the coming age
Shy deer and hounds together come to drink.

"Begin, my flute, with me Maenalian lays.
Now, Mopsus, cut new torches, for they bring
Your bride along; now, bridegroom, scatter nuts:
Forsaking Oeta mounts the evening star!

"Begin, my flute, with me Maenalian lays.
O worthy of thy mate, while all men else
Thou scornest, and with loathing dost behold
My shepherd's pipe, my goats, my shaggy brow,
And untrimmed beard, nor deem'st that any god
For mortal doings hath regard or care.

"Begin, my flute, with me Maenalian lays.
Once with your mother, in our orchard-garth,
A little maid I saw you—I your guide—
Plucking the dewy apples. My twelfth year
I scarce had entered, and could barely reach
The brittle boughs. I looked, and I was lost;
A sudden frenzy swept my wits away.

"Begin, my flute, with me Maenalian lays.
Now know I what Love is: 'mid savage rocks
Tmaros or Rhodope brought forth the boy,
Or Garamantes in earth's utmost bounds—
No kin of ours, nor of our blood begot.

"Begin, my flute, with me Maenalian lays.
Fierce Love it was once steeled a mother's heart
With her own offspring's blood her hands to imbrue:
Mother, thou too wert cruel; say wert thou
More cruel, mother, or more ruthless he?
Ruthless the boy, thou, mother, cruel too.

"Begin, my flute, with me Maenalian lays.
Now let the wolf turn tail and fly the sheep,
Tough oaks bear golden apples, alder-trees
Bloom with narcissus-flower, the tamarisk
Sweat with rich amber, and the screech-owl vie

In singing with the swan: let Tityrus
Be Orpheus, Orpheus in the forest-glade,
Arion 'mid his dolphins on the deep.

   "Begin, my flute, with me Maenalian lays.
Yea, be the whole earth to mid-ocean turned!
Farewell, ye woodlands! I from the tall peak
Of yon aerial rock will headlong plunge
Into the billows: this my latest gift,
From dying lips bequeathed thee, see thou keep.
Cease now, my flute, now cease Maenalian lays."

   Thus Damon: but do ye, Pierian Maids—
We cannot all do all things—tell me how
Alphesiboeus to his strain replied.

A.    "Bring water, and with soft wool-fillet bind
These altars round about, and burn thereon
Rich vervain and male frankincense, that I
May strive with magic spells to turn astray
My lover's saner senses, whereunto
There lacketh nothing save the power of song.

   "Draw from the town, my songs, draw Daphnis home.
Songs can the very moon draw down from heaven
Circe with singing changed from human form
The comrades of Ulysses, and by song
Is the cold meadow-snake, asunder burst.

   "Draw from the town, my songs, draw Daphnis home.
These triple threads of threefold colour first
I twine about thee, and three times withal
Around these altars do thine image bear:
Uneven numbers are the god's delight.

   "Draw from the town, my songs, draw Daphnis home.
Now, Amaryllis, ply in triple knots
The threefold colours; ply them fast, and say
This is the chain of Venus that I ply.

   "Draw from the town, my songs, draw Daphnis home.
As by the kindling of the self-same fire
Harder this clay, this wax the softer grows,
So by my love may Daphnis; sprinkle meal,
And with bitumen burn the brittle bays.
Me Daphnis with his cruelty doth burn,
I to melt cruel Daphnis burn this bay.

   "Draw from the town, my songs, draw Daphnis home.
As when some heifer, seeking for her steer
Through woodland and deep grove, sinks wearied out

On the green sedge beside a stream, love-lorn,
Nor marks the gathering night that calls her home—
As pines that heifer, with such love as hers
May Daphnis pine, and I not care to heal.

    "Draw from the town, my songs, draw Daphnis home.
These relics once, dear pledges of himself,
The traitor left me, which, O earth, to thee
Here on this very threshold I commit—
Pledges that bind him to redeem the debt.

    "Draw from the town, my songs, draw Daphnis home.
These herbs of bane to me did Moeris give,
In Pontus culled, where baneful herbs abound.
With these full oft have I seen Moeris change
To a wolf's form, and hide him in the woods,
Oft summon spirits from the tomb's recess,
And to new fields transport the standing corn.

    "Draw from the town, my songs, draw Daphnis home.
Take ashes, Amaryllis, fetch them forth,
And o'er your head into the running brook
Fling them, nor look behind: with these will I
Upon the heart of Daphnis make essay.
Nothing for gods, nothing for songs cares he.

    "Draw from the town, my songs, draw Daphnis home.
Look, look! the very embers of themselves
Have caught the altar with a flickering flame,
While I delay to fetch them: may the sign
Prove lucky! something it must mean, for sure,
And Hylax on the threshold 'gins to bark!
May we believe it, or are lovers still
By their own fancies fooled?
                         Give o'er, my songs,
Daphnis is coming from the town, give o'er."

# ECLOGUE IX

## LYCIDAS. MOERIS.

L.    Say whither, Moeris?—Make you for the town,
      Or on what errand bent?

M.                  O Lycidas,
      We have lived to see, what never yet we feared,
      An interloper own our little farm,
      And say, "Be off, you former husbandmen!
      These fields are mine." Now, cowed and out of heart,
      Since Fortune turns the whole world upside down,
      We are taking him—ill luck go with the same!—
      These kids you see.

L.                But surely I had heard
      That where the hills first draw from off the plain,
      And the high ridge with gentle slope descends,
      Down to the brook-side and the broken crests
      Of yonder veteran beeches, all the land
      Was by the songs of your Menalcas saved.

M.    Heard it you had, and so the rumour ran,
      But 'mid the clash of arms, my Lycidas,
      Our songs avail no more than, as 'tis said,
      Doves of Dodona when an eagle comes.
      Nay, had I not, from hollow ilex-bole
      Warned by a raven on the left, cut short
      The rising feud, nor I, your Moeris here,
      No, nor Menalcas, were alive to-day.

L.    Alack! could any of so foul a crime
      Be guilty? Ah! how nearly, thyself,
      Reft was the solace that we had in thee,
      Menalcas! Who then of the Nymphs had sung,
      Or who with flowering herbs bestrewn the ground,

And o'er the fountains drawn a leafy veil?—
Who sung the stave I filched from you that day
To Amaryllis wending, our hearts' joy?—
"While I am gone, 'tis but a little way,
Feed, Tityrus, my goats, and, having fed,
Drive to the drinking-pool, and, as you drive,
Beware the he-goat; with his horn he butts."

M.    Ay, or to Varus that half-finished lay,
"Varus, thy name, so still our Mantua live—
Mantua to poor Cremona all too near—
Shall singing swans bear upward to the stars."

L.    So may your swarms Cyrnean yew-trees shun,
Your kine with Cytisus their udders swell,
Begin, if aught you have. The Muses made
Me too a singer; I too have sung; the swains
Call me a poet, but I believe them not:
For naught of mine, or worthy Varius yet
Or Cinna deem I, but account myself
A cackling goose among melodious swans.

M.    'Twas in my thought to do so, Lycidas;
Even now was I revolving silently
If this I could recall—no paltry song:
"Come, Galatea, what pleasure is 't to play
Amid the waves? Here glows the Spring, here earth
Beside the streams pours forth a thousand flowers;
Here the white poplar bends above the cave,
And the lithe vine weaves shadowy covert: come,
Leave the mad waves to beat upon the shore."

L.    What of the strain I heard you singing once
On a clear night alone? the notes I still
Remember, could I but recall the words.

M.    "Why, Daphnis, upward gazing, do you mark
The ancient risings of the Signs? for look
Where Dionean Caesar's star comes forth
In heaven, to gladden all the fields with corn,
And to the grape upon the sunny slopes
Her colour bring! Now, Daphnis, graft the pears;
So shall your children's children pluck their fruit.
    Time carries all things, even our wits, away.
Oft, as a boy, I sang the sun to rest,
But all those songs are from my memory fled,
And even his voice is failing Moeris now;
The wolves eyed Moeris first: but at your wish

Menalcas will repeat them oft enow.

L.     Your pleas but linger out my heart's desire:
Now all the deep is into silence hushed,
And all the murmuring breezes sunk to sleep.
We are half-way thither, for Bianor's tomb
Begins to show: here, Moeris, where the hinds
Are lopping the thick leafage, let us sing.
Set down the kids, yet shall we reach the town;
Or, if we fear the night may gather rain
Ere we arrive, then singing let us go,
Our way to lighten; and, that we may thus
Go singing, I will ease you of this load.

M.    Cease, boy, and get we to the work in hand:
We shall sing better when himself is come.

# ECLOGUE X

## GALLUS.

This now, the very latest of my toils,
Vouchsafe me, Arethusa! needs must I
Sing a brief song to Gallus—brief, but yet
Such as Lycoris' self may fitly read.
Who would not sing for Gallus? So, when thou
Beneath Sicanian billows glidest on,
May Doris blend no bitter wave with thine,
Begin! The love of Gallus be our theme,
And the shrewd pangs he suffered, while, hard by,
The flat-nosed she-goats browse the tender brush.
We sing not to deaf ears; no word of ours
But the woods echo it. What groves or lawns
Held you, ye Dryad-maidens, when for love—
Love all unworthy of a loss so dear—
Gallus lay dying? for neither did the slopes
Of Pindus or Parnassus stay you then,
No, nor Aonian Aganippe. Him
Even the laurels and the tamarisks wept;
For him, outstretched beneath a lonely rock,
Wept pine-clad Maenalus, and the flinty crags
Of cold Lycaeus. The sheep too stood around—
Of us they feel no shame, poet divine;
Nor of the flock be thou ashamed: even fair
Adonis by the rivers fed his sheep—
Came shepherd too, and swine-herd footing slow,
And, from the winter-acorns dripping-wet
Menalcas. All with one accord exclaim:
"From whence this love of thine?" Apollo came;
"Gallus, art mad?" he cried, "thy bosom's care

30

Another love is following." Therewithal
Silvanus came, with rural honours crowned;
The flowering fennels and tall lilies shook
Before him. Yea, and our own eyes beheld
Pan, god of Arcady, with blood-red juice
Of the elder-berry, and with vermilion, dyed.
"Wilt ever make an end?" quoth he, "behold
Love recks not aught of it: his heart no more
With tears is sated than with streams the grass,
Bees with the cytisus, or goats with leaves."
"Yet will ye sing, Arcadians, of my woes
Upon your mountains," sadly he replied—
"Arcadians, that alone have skill to sing.
O then how softly would my ashes rest,
If of my love, one day, your flutes should tell!
And would that I, of your own fellowship,
Or dresser of the ripening grape had been,
Or guardian of the flock! for surely then,
Let Phyllis, or Amyntas, or who else,
Bewitch me—what if swart Amyntas be?
Dark is the violet, dark the hyacinth—
Among the willows, 'neath the limber vine,
Reclining would my love have lain with me,
Phyllis plucked garlands, or Amyntas sung.
Here are cool springs, soft mead and grove, Lycoris;
Here might our lives with time have worn away.
But me mad love of the stern war-god holds
Armed amid weapons and opposing foes.
Whilst thou—Ah! might I but believe it not!—
Alone without me, and from home afar,
Look'st upon Alpine snows and frozen Rhine.
Ah! may the frost not hurt thee, may the sharp
And jaggèd ice not wound thy tender feet!
I will depart, re-tune the songs I framed
In verse Chalcidian to the oaten reed
Of the Sicilian swain. Resolved am I
In the woods, rather, with wild beasts to couch,
And bear my doom, and character my love
Upon the tender tree-trunks: they will grow,
And you, my love, grow with them. And meanwhile
I with the Nymphs will haunt Mount Maenalus,
Or hunt the keen wild boar. No frost so cold
But I will hem with hounds thy forest-glades,

Parthenius. Even now, methinks, I range
O'er rocks, through echoing groves, and joy to launch
Cydonian arrows from a Parthian bow.—
As if my madness could find healing thus,
Or that god soften at a mortal's grief!
Now neither Hamadryads, no, nor songs
Delight me more: ye woods, away with you!
No pangs of ours can change him; not though we
In the mid-frost should drink of Hebrus' stream,
And in wet winters face Sithonian snows,
Or, when the bark of the tall elm-tree bole
Of drought is dying, should, under Cancer's Sign,
In Aethiopian deserts drive our flocks.
Love conquers all things; yield we too to love!"
    These songs, Pierian Maids, shall it suffice
Your poet to have sung, the while he sat,
And of slim mallow wove a basket fine:
To Gallus ye will magnify their worth,
Gallus, for whom my love grows hour by hour,
As the green alder shoots in early Spring.
Come, let us rise: the shade is wont to be
Baneful to singers; baneful is the shade
Cast by the juniper, crops sicken too
In shade. Now homeward, having fed your fill—
Eve's star is rising—go, my she-goats, go.

# THE GEORGICS

κείνης τ᾽ ἐκεῖθεν τοῦτο τοῦ ζῶντος τ᾽ ἐμοῦ
δῶρον φέρω σοὶ μητρὶ τῶν ἀμητόρων.

# GEORGIC I

What makes the cornfield smile; beneath what star
Maecenas, it is meet to turn the sod
Or marry elm with vine; how tend the steer;
What pains for cattle-keeping, or what proof
Of patient trial serves for thrifty bees;—
Such are my themes.
                O universal lights
Most glorious! ye that lead the gliding year
Along the sky, Liber and Ceres mild,
If by your bounty holpen earth once changed
Chaonian acorn for the plump wheat-ear,
And mingled with the grape, your new-found gift,
The draughts of Achelous; and ye Fauns
To rustics ever kind, come foot it, Fauns
And Dryad-maids together; your gifts I sing.
And thou, for whose delight the war-horse first
Sprang from earth's womb at thy great trident's stroke,
Neptune; and haunter of the groves, for whom
Three hundred snow-white heifers browse the brakes,
The fertile brakes of Ceos; and clothed in power,
Thy native forest and Lycean lawns,
Pan, shepherd-god, forsaking, as the love
Of thine own Maenalus constrains thee, hear
And help, O lord of Tegea! And thou, too,
Minerva, from whose hand the olive sprung;
And boy-discoverer of the curvèd plough;
And, bearing a young cypress root-uptorn,
Silvanus, and Gods all and Goddesses,
Who make the fields your care, both ye who nurse
The tender unsown increase, and from heaven
Shed on man's sowing the riches of your rain:

And thou, even thou, of whom we know not yet
What mansion of the skies shall hold thee soon,
Whether to watch o'er cities be thy will,
Great Caesar, and to take the earth in charge,
That so the mighty world may welcome thee
Lord of her increase, master of her times,
Binding thy mother's myrtle round thy brow,
Or as the boundless ocean's God thou come,
Sole dread of seamen, till far Thule bow
Before thee, and Tethys win thee to her son
With all her waves for dower; or as a star
Lend thy fresh beams our lagging months to cheer,
Where 'twixt the Maid and those pursuing Claws
A space is opening; see! red Scorpio's self
His arms draws in, yea, and hath left thee more
Than thy full meed of heaven: be what thou wilt—
For neither Tartarus hopes to call thee king,
Nor may so dire a lust of sovereignty
E'er light upon thee, howso Greece admire
Elysium's fields, and Proserpine not heed
Her mother's voice entreating to return—
Vouchsafe a prosperous voyage, and smile on this
My bold endeavour, and pitying, even as I,
These poor way-wildered swains, at once begin,
Grow timely used unto the voice of prayer.

   In early spring-tide, when the icy drip
Melts from the mountains hoar, and Zephyr's breath
Unbinds the crumbling clod, even then 'tis time;
Press deep your plough behind the groaning ox,
And teach the furrow-burnished share to shine.
That land the craving farmer's prayer fulfils,
Which twice the sunshine, twice the frost has felt;
Ay, that's the land whose boundless harvest-crops
Burst, see! the barns.

                  But ere our metal cleave
An unknown surface, heed we to forelearn
The winds and varying temper of the sky,
The lineal tilth and habits of the spot,
What every region yields, and what denies.
Here blithelier springs the corn, and here the grape,
There earth is green with tender growth of trees
And grass unbidden. See how from Tmolus comes
The saffron's fragrance, ivory from Ind,

From Saba's weakling sons their frankincense,
Iron from the naked Chalybs, castor rank
From Pontus, from Epirus the prize-palms
O' the mares of Elis.
                    Such the eternal bond
And such the laws by Nature's hand imposed
On clime and clime, e'er since the primal dawn
When old Deucalion on the unpeopled earth
Cast stones, whence men, a flinty race, were reared.
Up then! if fat the soil, let sturdy bulls
Upturn it from the year's first opening months,
And let the clods lie bare till baked to dust
By the ripe suns of summer; but if the earth
Less fruitful be, just ere Arcturus rise
With shallower trench uptilt it—'twill suffice;
There, lest weeds choke the crop's luxuriance, here,
Lest the scant moisture fail the barren sand.

    Then thou shalt suffer in alternate years
The new-reaped fields to rest, and on the plain
A crust of sloth to harden; or, when stars
Are changed in heaven, there sow the golden grain
Where erst, luxuriant with its quivering pod,
Pulse, or the slender vetch-crop, thou hast cleared,
And lupin sour, whose brittle stalks arise,
A hurtling forest. For the plain is parched
By flax-crop, parched by oats, by poppies parched
In Lethe-slumber drenched. Nathless by change
The travailing earth is lightened, but stint not
With refuse rich to soak the thirsty soil,
And shower foul ashes o'er the exhausted fields.
Thus by rotation like repose is gained,
Nor earth meanwhile uneared and thankless left.
Oft, too, 'twill boot to fire the naked fields,
And the light stubble burn with crackling flames;
Whether that earth therefrom some hidden strength
And fattening food derives, or that the fire
Bakes every blemish out, and sweats away
Each useless humour, or that the heat unlocks
New passages and secret pores, whereby
Their life-juice to the tender blades may win;
Or that it hardens more and helps to bind
The gaping veins, lest penetrating showers,
Or fierce sun's ravening might, or searching blast

Of the keen north should sear them. Well, I wot,
He serves the fields who with his harrow breaks
The sluggish clods, and hurdles osier-twined
Hales o'er them; from the far Olympian height
Him golden Ceres not in vain regards;
And he, who having ploughed the fallow plain
And heaved its furrowy ridges, turns once more
Cross-wise his shattering share, with stroke on stroke
The earth assails, and makes the field his thrall.
   Pray for wet summers and for winters fine,
Ye husbandmen; in winter's dust the crops
Exceedingly rejoice, the field hath joy;
No tilth makes Mysia lift her head so high,
Nor Gargarus his own harvests so admire.
Why tell of him, who, having launched his seed,
Sets on for close encounter, and rakes smooth
The dry dust hillocks, then on the tender corn
Lets in the flood, whose waters follow fain;
And when the parched field quivers, and all the blades
Are dying, from the brow of its hill-bed,
See! see! he lures the runnel; down it falls,
Waking hoarse murmurs o'er the polished stones,
And with its bubblings slakes the thirsty fields?
Or why of him, who lest the heavy ears
O'erweigh the stalk, while yet in tender blade
Feeds down the crop's luxuriance, when its growth
First tops the furrows? Why of him who drains
The marsh-land's gathered ooze through soaking sand,
Chiefly what time in treacherous moons a stream
Goes out in spate, and with its coat of slime
Holds all the country, whence the hollow dykes
Sweat steaming vapour?
                       But no whit the more,
For all expedients tried and travail borne
By man and beast in turning oft the soil,
Do greedy goose and Strymon-haunting cranes
And succory's bitter fibres cease to harm,
Or shade not injure. The great Sire himself
No easy road to husbandry assigned,
And first was he by human skill to rouse
The slumbering glebe, whetting the minds of men
With care on care, nor suffering realm of his
In drowsy sloth to stagnate. Before Jove

Fields knew no taming hand of husbandmen;
To mark the plain or mete with boundary-line—
Even this was impious; for the common stock
They gathered, and the earth of her own will
All things more freely, no man bidding, bore.
He to black serpents gave their venom-bane,
And bade the wolf go prowl, and ocean toss;
Shook from the leaves their honey, put fire away,
And curbed the random rivers running wine,
That use by gradual dint of thought on thought
Might forge the various arts, with furrow's help
The corn-blade win, and strike out hidden fire
From the flint's heart. Then first the streams were ware
Of hollowed alder-hulls: the sailor then
Their names and numbers gave to star and star,
Pleiads and Hyads, and Lycaon's child
Bright Arctos; how with nooses then was found
To catch wild beasts, and cozen them with lime,
And hem with hounds the mighty forest-glades.
Soon one with hand-net scourges the broad stream,
Probing its depths, one drags his dripping toils
Along the main; then iron's unbending might,
And shrieking saw-blade,—for the men of old
With wedges wont to cleave the splintering log;—
Then divers arts arose; toil conquered all,
Remorseless toil, and poverty's shrewd push
In times of hardship. Ceres was the first
Set mortals on with tools to turn the sod,
When now the awful groves 'gan fail to bear
Acorns and arbutes, and her wonted food
Dodona gave no more. Soon, too, the corn
Gat sorrow's increase, that an evil blight
Ate up the stalks, and thistle reared his spines
An idler in the fields; the crops die down;
Upsprings instead a shaggy growth of burrs
And caltrops; and amid the corn-fields trim
Unfruitful darnel and wild oats have sway.
Wherefore, unless thou shalt with ceaseless rake
The weeds pursue, with shouting scare the birds,
Prune with thy hook the dark field's matted shade,
Pray down the showers, all vainly thou shalt eye,
Alack! thy neighbour's heaped-up harvest-mow,
And in the greenwood from a shaken oak

Seek solace for thine hunger.
                                    Now to tell
The sturdy rustics' weapons, what they are,
Without which, neither can be sown nor reared
The fruits of harvest; first the bent plough's share
And heavy timber, and slow-lumbering wains
Of the Eleusinian mother, threshing-sleighs
And drags, and harrows with their crushing weight;
Then the cheap wicker-ware of Celeus old,
Hurdles of arbute, and thy mystic fan,
Iacchus; which, full tale, long ere the time
Thou must with heed lay by, if thee await
Not all unearned the country's crown divine.
While yet within the woods, the elm is tamed
And bowed with mighty force to form the stock,
And take the plough's curved shape, then nigh the root
A pole eight feet projecting, earth-boards twain,
And share-beam with its double back they fix.
For yoke is early hewn a linden light,
And a tall beech for handle, from behind
To turn the car at lowest: then o'er the hearth
The wood they hang till the smoke knows it well.
   Many the precepts of the men of old
I can recount thee, so thou start not back,
And such slight cares to learn not weary thee.
And this among the first: thy threshing-floor
With ponderous roller must be levelled smooth,
And wrought by hand, and fixed with binding chalk,
Lest weeds arise, or dust a passage win
Splitting the surface, then a thousand plagues
Make sport of it: oft builds the tiny mouse
Her home, and plants her granary, underground,
Or burrow for their bed the purblind moles,
Or toad is found in hollows, and all the swarm
Of earth's unsightly creatures; or a huge
Corn-heap the weevil plunders, and the ant,
Fearful of coming age and penury.
   Mark too, what time the walnut in the woods
With ample bloom shall clothe her, and bow down
Her odorous branches, if the fruit prevail,
Like store of grain will follow, and there shall come
A mighty winnowing-time with mighty heat;
But if the shade with wealth of leaves abound.

Vainly your threshing-floor will bruise the stalks
Rich but in chaff. Many myself have seen
Steep, as they sow, their pulse-seeds, drenching them
With nitre and black oil-lees, that the fruit
Might swell within the treacherous pods, and they
Make speed to boil at howso small a fire.
Yet, culled with caution, proved with patient toil,
These have I seen degenerate, did not man
Put forth his hand with power, and year by year
Choose out the largest. So, by fate impelled,
Speed all things to the worse, and backward borne
Glide from us; even as who with struggling oars
Up stream scarce pulls a shallop, if he chance
His arms to slacken, lo! with headlong force
The current sweeps him down the hurrying tide.

   Us too behoves Arcturus' sign observe,
And the Kids' seasons and the shining Snake,
No less than those who o'er the windy main
Borne homeward tempt the Pontic, and the jaws
Of oyster-rife Abydos. When the Scales
Now poising fair the hours of sleep and day
Give half the world to sunshine, half to shade,
Then urge your bulls, my masters; sow the plain
Even to the verge of tameless winter's showers
With barley: then, too, time it is to hide
Your flax in earth, and poppy, Ceres' joy,
Aye, more than time to bend above the plough,
While earth, yet dry, forbids not, and the clouds
Are buoyant. With the spring comes bean-sowing;
Thee, too, Lucerne, the crumbling furrows then
Receive, and millet's annual care returns,
What time the white bull with his gilded horns
Opens the year, before whose threatening front,
Routed the dog-star sinks. But if it be
For wheaten harvest and the hardy spelt,
Thou tax the soil, to corn-ears wholly given,
Let Atlas' daughters hide them in the dawn,
The Cretan star, a crown of fire, depart,
Or e'er the furrow's claim of seed thou quit,
Or haste thee to entrust the whole year's hope
To earth that would not. Many have begun
Ere Maia's star be setting; these, I trow,
Their looked-for harvest fools with empty ears.

But if the vetch and common kidney-bean
Thou'rt fain to sow, nor scorn to make thy care
Pelusiac lentil, no uncertain sign
Boötes' fall will send thee; then begin,
Pursue thy sowing till half the frosts be done.
　　Therefore it is the golden sun, his course
Into fixed parts dividing, rules his way
Through the twelve constellations of the world.
Five zones the heavens contain; whereof is one
Aye red with flashing sunlight, fervent aye
From fire; on either side to left and right
Are traced the utmost twain, stiff with blue ice,
And black with scowling storm-clouds, and betwixt
These and the midmost, other twain there lie,
By the Gods' grace to heart-sick mortals given,
And a path cleft between them, where might wheel
On sloping plane the system of the Signs.
And as toward Scythia and Rhipaean heights
The world mounts upward, likewise sinks it down
Toward Libya and the south, this pole of ours
Still towering high, that other, 'neath their feet,
By dark Styx frowned on, and the abysmal shades.
Here glides the huge Snake forth with sinuous coils
'Twixt the two Bears and round them river-wise—
The Bears that fear 'neath Ocean's brim to dip.
There either, say they, reigns the eternal hush
Of night that knows no seasons, her black pall
Thick-mantling fold on fold; or thitherward
From us returning Dawn brings back the day;
And when the first breath of his panting steeds
On us the Orient flings, that hour with them
Red Vesper 'gins to trim his 'lated fires.
Hence under doubtful skies forebode we can
The coming tempests, hence both harvest-day
And seed-time, when to smite the treacherous main
With driving oars, when launch the fair-rigged fleet,
Or in ripe hour to fell the forest-pine.
Hence, too, not idly do we watch the stars—
Their rising and their setting—and the year,
Four varying seasons to one law conformed.
　　If chilly showers e'er shut the farmer's door,
Much that had soon with sunshine cried for haste,
He may forestall; the ploughman batters keen

His blunted share's hard tooth, scoops from a tree
His troughs, or on the cattle stamps a brand,
Or numbers on the corn-heaps; some make sharp
The stakes and two-pronged forks, and willow-bands
Amerian for the bending vine prepare.
Now let the pliant basket plaited be
Of bramble-twigs; now set your corn to parch
Before the fire; now bruise it with the stone.
Nay even on holy days some tasks to ply
Is right and lawful: this no ban forbids,
To turn the runnel's course, fence corn-fields in,
Make springes for the birds, burn up the briars,
And plunge in wholesome stream the bleating flock.
Oft too with oil or apples plenty-cheap
The creeping ass's ribs his driver packs,
And home from town returning brings instead
A dented mill-stone or black lump of pitch.

   The moon herself in various rank assigns
The days for labour lucky: fly the fifth;
Then sprang pale Orcus and the Eumenides;
Earth then in awful labour brought to light
Coeus, Iapetus, and Typhöeus fell,
And those sworn brethren banded to break down
The gates of heaven; thrice, sooth to say, they strove
Ossa on Pelion's top to heave and heap,
Aye, and on Ossa to up-roll amain
Leafy Olympus; thrice with thunderbolt
Their mountain-stair the Sire asunder smote.
Seventh after tenth is lucky both to set
The vine in earth, and take and tame the steer,
And fix the leashes to the warp; the ninth
To runagates is kinder, cross to thieves.

   Many the tasks that lightlier lend themselves
In chilly night, or when the sun is young,
And Dawn bedews the world. By night 'tis best
To reap light stubble, and parched fields by night;
For nights the suppling moisture never fails.
And one will sit the long late watches out
By winter fire-light, shaping with keen blade
The torches to a point; his wife the while,
Her tedious labour soothing with a song,
Speeds the shrill comb along the warp, or else
With Vulcan's aid boils the sweet must-juice down,

And skims with leaves the quivering cauldron's wave.
  But ruddy Ceres in mid heat is mown,
And in mid heat the parchèd ears are bruised
Upon the floor; to plough strip, strip to sow;
Winter's the lazy time for husbandmen.
In the cold season farmers wont to taste
The increase of their toil, and yield themselves
To mutual interchange of festal cheer.
Boon winter bids them, and unbinds their cares,
As laden keels, when now the port they touch,
And happy sailors crown the sterns with flowers.
Nathless then also time it is to strip
Acorns from oaks, and berries from the bay,
Olives, and bleeding myrtles, then to set
Snares for the crane, and meshes for the stag,
And hunt the long-eared hares, then pierce the doe
With whirl of hempen-thonged Balearic sling,
While snow lies deep, and streams are drifting ice.
  What need to tell of autumn's storms and stars,
And wherefore men must watch, when now the day
Grows shorter, and more soft the summer's heat?
When Spring the rain-bringer comes rushing down,
Or when the beards of harvest on the plain
Bristle already, and the milky corn
On its green stalk is swelling? Many a time,
When now the farmer to his yellow fields
The reaping-hind came bringing, even in act
To lop the brittle barley stems, have I
Seen all the windy legions clash in war
Together, as to rend up far and wide
The heavy corn-crop from its lowest roots,
And toss it skyward: so might winter's flaw,
Dark-eddying, whirl light stalks and flying straws.
  Oft too comes looming vast along the sky
A march of waters; mustering from above,
The clouds roll up the tempest, heaped and grim
With angry showers: down falls the height of heaven,
And with a great rain floods the smiling crops,
The oxen's labour: now the dikes fill fast,
And the void river-beds swell thunderously,
And all the panting firths of Ocean boil.
The Sire himself in midnight of the clouds
Wields with red hand the levin; through all her bulk

Earth at the hurly quakes; the beasts are fled,
And mortal hearts of every kindred sunk
In cowering terror; he with flaming brand
Athos, or Rhodope, or Ceraunian crags
Precipitates: then doubly raves the South
With shower on blinding shower, and woods and coasts
Wail fitfully beneath the mighty blast.
This fearing, mark the months and Signs of heaven,
Whither retires him Saturn's icy star,
And through what heavenly cycles wandereth
The glowing orb Cyllenian. Before all
Worship the Gods, and to great Ceres pay
Her yearly dues upon the happy sward
With sacrifice, anigh the utmost end
Of winter, and when Spring begins to smile.
Then lambs are fat, and wines are mellowest then:
Then sleep is sweet, and dark the shadows fall
Upon the mountains. Let your rustic youth
To Ceres do obeisance, one and all;
And for her pleasure thou mix honeycombs
With milk and the ripe wine-god; thrice for luck
Around the young corn let the victim go,
And all the choir, a joyful company,
Attend it, and with shouts bid Ceres come
To be their house-mate; and let no man dare
Put sickle to the ripened ears until,
With woven oak his temples chapleted,
He foot the ruggèd dance and chant the lay.
   Aye, and that these things we might win to know
By certain tokens, heats, and showers, and winds
That bring the frost, the Sire of all himself
Ordained what warnings in her monthly round
The moon should give, what bodes the south wind's fall,
What oft-repeated sights the herdsman seeing
Should keep his cattle closer to their stalls.
No sooner are the winds at point to rise,
Than either Ocean's firths begin to toss
And swell, and a dry crackling sound is heard
Upon the heights, or one loud ferment booms
The beach afar, and through the forest goes
A murmur multitudinous. By this
Scarce can the billow spare the curvèd keels,
When swift the sea-gulls from the middle main

Come winging, and their shrieks are shoreward borne,
When ocean-loving cormorants on dry land
Besport them, and the hern, her marshy haunts
Forsaking, mounts above the soaring cloud.
Oft, too, when wind is toward, the stars thou'lt see
From heaven shoot headlong, and through murky night
Long trails of fire white-glistening in their wake,
Or light chaff flit in air with fallen leaves,
Or feathers on the wave-top float and play.
But when from regions of the furious North
It lightens, and when thunder fills the halls
Of Eurus and of Zephyr, all the fields
With brimming dikes are flooded, and at sea
No mariner but furls his dripping sails.
Never at unawares did shower annoy:
Or, as it rises, the high-soaring cranes
Flee to the vales before it, or, with face
Upturned to heaven, the heifer snuffs the gale
Through gaping nostrils, or about the meres
Shrill-twittering flits the swallow, and the frogs
Crouch in the mud and chant their dirge of old.
Oft, too, the ant from out her inmost cells,
Fretting the narrow path, her eggs conveys;
Or the huge bow sucks moisture; or a host
Of rooks from food returning in long line
Clamour with jostling wings. Now mayst thou see
The various ocean-fowl and those that pry
Round Asian meads within thy freshet-pools,
Cayster, as in eager rivalry,
About their shoulders dash the plenteous spray,
Now duck their head beneath the wave, now run
Into the billows, for sheer idle joy
Of their mad bathing-revel. Then the crow
With full voice, good-for-naught, inviting rain,
Stalks on the dry sand mateless and alone.
Nor e'en the maids, that card their nightly task,
Know not the storm-sign, when in blazing crock
They see the lamp-oil sputtering with a growth
Of mouldy snuff-clots.
                    So too, after rain,
Sunshine and open skies thou mayst forecast,
And learn by tokens sure, for then nor dimmed
Appear the stars' keen edges, nor the moon

As borrowing of her brother's beams to rise,
Nor fleecy films to float along the sky.
Not to the sun's warmth then upon the shore
Do halcyons dear to Thetis ope their wings,
Nor filthy swine take thought to toss on high
With scattering snout the straw-wisps. But the clouds
Seek more the vales, and rest upon the plain,
And from the roof-top the night-owl for naught
Watching the sunset plies her 'lated song.
Distinct in clearest air is Nisus seen
Towering, and Scylla for the purple lock
Pays dear; for whereso, as she flies, her wings
The light air winnow, lo! fierce, implacable,
Nisus with mighty whirr through heaven pursues;
Where Nisus heavenward soareth, there her wings
Clutch as she flies, the light air winnowing still.
Soft then the voice of rooks from indrawn throat
Thrice, four times, o'er repeated, and full oft
On their high cradles, by some hidden joy
Gladdened beyond their wont, in bustling throngs
Among the leaves they riot; so sweet it is,
When showers are spent, their own loved nests again
And tender brood to visit. Not, I deem,
That heaven some native wit to these assigned,
Or fate a larger prescience, but that when
The storm and shifting moisture of the air
Have changed their courses, and the sky-god now,
Wet with the south-wind, thickens what was rare,
And what was gross releases, then, too, change
Their spirits' fleeting phases, and their breasts
Feel other motions now, than when the wind
Was driving up the cloud-rack. Hence proceeds
That blending of the feathered choirs afield,
The cattle's exultation, and the rooks'
Deep-throated triumph.
                              But if the headlong sun
And moons in order following thou regard,
Ne'er will to-morrow's hour deceive thee, ne'er
Wilt thou be caught by guile of cloudless night.
When first the moon recalls her rallying fires,
If dark the air clipped by her crescent dim,
For folks afield and on the open sea
A mighty rain is brewing; but if her face

With maiden blush she mantle, 'twill be wind,
For wind turns Phoebe still to ruddier gold.
But if at her fourth rising, for 'tis that
Gives surest counsel, clear she ride thro' heaven
With horns unblunted, then shall that whole day,
And to the month's end those that spring from it,
Rainless and windless be, while safe ashore
Shall sailors pay their vows to Panope,
Glaucus, and Melicertes, Ino's child.
   The sun too, both at rising, and when soon
He dives beneath the waves, shall yield thee signs;
For signs, none trustier, travel with the sun,
Both those which in their course with dawn he brings,
And those at star-rise. When his springing orb
With spots he pranketh, muffled in a cloud,
And shrinks mid-circle, then of showers beware;
For then the South comes driving from the deep,
To trees and crops and cattle bringing bane.
Or when at day-break through dark clouds his rays
Burst and are scattered, or when rising pale
Aurora quits Tithonus' saffron bed,
But sorry shelter then, alack! will yield
Vine-leaf to ripening grapes; so thick a hail
In spiky showers spins rattling on the roof.
And this yet more 'twill boot thee bear in mind,
When now, his course upon Olympus run,
He draws to his decline: for oft we see
Upon the sun's own face strange colours stray;
Dark tells of rain, of east winds fiery-red;
If spots with ruddy fire begin to mix,
Then all the heavens convulsed in wrath thou'lt see—
Storm-clouds and wind together. Me that night
Let no man bid fare forth upon the deep,
Nor rend the rope from shore. But if, when both
He brings again and hides the day's return,
Clear-orbed he shineth, idly wilt thou dread
The storm-clouds, and beneath the lustral North
See the woods waving. What late eve in fine
Bears in her bosom, whence the wind that brings
Fair-weather-clouds, or what the rainy South
Is meditating, tokens of all these
The sun will give thee. Who dare charge the sun
With leasing? He it is who warneth oft

Of hidden broils at hand and treachery,
And secret swelling of the waves of war.
He too it was, when Caesar's light was quenched,
For Rome had pity, when his bright head he veiled
In iron-hued darkness, till a godless age
Trembled for night eternal; at that time
Howbeit earth also, and the ocean-plains,
And dogs obscene, and birds of evil bode
Gave tokens. Yea, how often have we seen
Etna, her furnace-walls asunder riven,
In billowy floods boil o'er the Cyclops' fields,
And roll down globes of fire and molten rocks!
A clash of arms through all the heaven was heard
By Germany; strange heavings shook the Alps.
Yea, and by many through the breathless groves
A voice was heard with power, and wondrous-pale
Phantoms were seen upon the dusk of night,
And cattle spake, portentous! streams stand still,
And the earth yawns asunder, ivory weeps
For sorrow in the shrines, and bronzes sweat.
Up-twirling forests with his eddying tide,
Madly he bears them down, that lord of floods,
Eridanus, till through all the plain are swept
Beasts and their stalls together. At that time
In gloomy entrails ceased not to appear
Dark-threatening fibres, springs to trickle blood,
And high-built cities night-long to resound
With the wolves' howling. Never more than then
From skies all cloudless fell the thunderbolts,
Nor blazed so oft the comet's fire of bale.
Therefore a second time Philippi saw
The Roman hosts with kindred weapons rush
To battle, nor did the high gods deem it hard
That twice Emathia and the wide champaign
Of Haemus should be fattening with our blood.
Ay, and the time will come when thereanigh,
Heaving the earth up with his curvèd plough,
Some swain will light on javelins by foul rust
Corroded, or with ponderous harrow strike
On empty helmets, while he gapes to see
Bones as of giants from the trench untombed.
Gods of my country, heroes of the soil,
And Romulus, and Mother Vesta, thou

Who Tuscan Tiber and Rome's Palatine
Preservest, this new champion at the least
Our fallen generation to repair
Forbid not. To the full and long ago
Our blood thy Trojan perjuries hath paid,
Laomedon. Long since the courts of heaven
Begrudge us thee, our Caesar, and complain
That thou regard'st the triumphs of mankind,
Here where the wrong is right, the right is wrong,
Where wars abound so many, and myriad-faced
Is crime; where no meet honour hath the plough;
The fields, their husbandmen led far away,
Rot in neglect, and curvèd pruning-hooks
Into the sword's stiff blade are fused and forged.
Euphrates here, here Germany new strife
Is stirring; neighbouring cities are in arms,
The laws that bound them snapped; and godless war
Rages through all the universe; as when
The four-horse chariots from the barriers poured
Still quicken o'er the course, and, idly now
Grasping the reins, the driver by his team
Is onward borne, nor heeds the car his curb.

# GEORGIC II

Thus far the tilth of fields and stars of heaven;
Now will I sing thee, Bacchus, and, with thee,
The forest's young plantations and the fruit
Of slow-maturing olive. Hither haste,
O Father of the wine-press; all things here
Teem with the bounties of thy hand; for thee
With viny autumn laden blooms the field,
And foams the vintage high with brimming vats;
Hither, O Father of the wine-press, come,
And stripped of buskin stain thy barèd limbs
In the new must with me.
                    First, nature's law
For generating trees is manifold;
For some of their own force spontaneous spring,
No hand of man compelling, and possess
The plains and river-windings far and wide,
As pliant osier and the bending broom,
Poplar, and willows in wan companies
With green leaf glimmering gray; and some there be
From chance-dropped seed that rear them, as the tall
Chestnuts, and, mightiest of the branching wood,
Jove's Aesculus, and oaks, oracular
Deemed by the Greeks of old. With some sprouts forth
A forest of dense suckers from the root,
As elms and cherries; so, too, a pigmy plant,
Beneath its mother's mighty shade upshoots
The bay-tree of Parnassus. Such the modes
Nature imparted first; hence all the race
Of forest-trees and shrubs and sacred groves
Springs into verdure.

Other means there are,
Which use by method for itself acquired.
One, sliving suckers from the tender frame
Of the tree-mother, plants them in the trench;
One buries the bare stumps within his field,
Truncheons cleft four-wise, or sharp-pointed stakes;
Some forest-trees the layer's bent arch await,
And slips yet quick within the parent-soil;
No root need others, nor doth the pruner's hand
Shrink to restore the topmost shoot to earth
That gave it being. Nay, marvellous to tell,
Lopped of its limbs, the olive, a mere stock,
Still thrusts its root out from the sapless wood,
And oft the branches of one kind we see
Change to another's with no loss to rue,
Pear-tree transformed the ingrafted apple yield,
And stony cornels on the plum-tree blush.
   Come then, and learn what tilth to each belongs
According to their kinds, ye husbandmen,
And tame with culture the wild fruits, lest earth
Lie idle. O blithe to make all Ismarus
One forest of the wine-god, and to clothe
With olives huge Tabernus! And be thou
At hand, and with me ply the voyage of toil
I am bound on, O my glory, O thou that art
Justly the chiefest portion of my fame,
Maecenas, and on this wide ocean launched
Spread sail like wings to waft thee. Not that I
With my poor verse would comprehend the whole,
Nay, though a hundred tongues, a hundred mouths
Were mine, a voice of iron; be thou at hand,
Skirt but the nearer coast-line; see the shore
Is in our grasp; not now with feignèd song
Through winding bouts and tedious preludings
Shall I detain thee.
                    Those that lift their head
Into the realms of light spontaneously,
Fruitless indeed, but blithe and strenuous spring,
Since Nature lurks within the soil. And yet
Even these, should one engraft them, or transplant
To well-drilled trenches, will anon put off
Their woodland temper, and, by frequent tilth,
To whatso craft thou summon them, make speed

To follow. So likewise will the barren shaft
That from the stock-root issueth, if it be
Set out with clear space amid open fields:
Now the tree-mother's towering leaves and boughs
Darken, despoil of increase as it grows,
And blast it in the bearing. Lastly, that
Which from shed seed ariseth, upward wins
But slowly, yielding promise of its shade
To late-born generations; apples wane
Forgetful of their former juice, the grape
Bears sorry clusters, for the birds a prey.

 Soothly on all must toil be spent, and all
Trained to the trench and at great cost subdued.
But reared from truncheons olives answer best,
As vines from layers, and from the solid wood
The Paphian myrtles; while from suckers spring
Both hardy hazels and huge ash, the tree
That rims with shade the brows of Hercules,
And acorns dear to the Chaonian sire:
So springs the towering palm too, and the fir
Destined to spy the dangers of the deep.
But the rough arbutus with walnut-fruit
Is grafted; so have barren planes ere now
Stout apples borne, with chestnut-flower the beech,
The mountain-ash with pear-bloom whitened o'er,
And swine crunched acorns 'neath the boughs of elms.

 Nor is the method of inserting eyes
And grafting one: for where the buds push forth
Amidst the bark, and burst the membranes thin,
Even on the knot a narrow rift is made,
Wherein from some strange tree a germ they pen,
And to the moist rind bid it cleave and grow.
Or, otherwise, in knotless trunks is hewn
A breach, and deep into the solid grain
A path with wedges cloven; then fruitful slips
Are set herein, and—no long time—behold!
To heaven upshot with teeming boughs, the tree
Strange leaves admires and fruitage not its own.

 Nor of one kind alone are sturdy elms,
Willow and lotus, nor the cypress-trees
Of Ida; nor of self-same fashion spring
Fat olives, orchades, and radii
And bitter-berried pausians, no, nor yet

Apples and the forests of Alcinous;
Nor from like cuttings are Crustumian pears
And Syrian, and the heavy hand-fillers.
Not the same vintage from our trees hangs down,
Which Lesbos from Methymna's tendril plucks.
Vines Thasian are there, Mareotids white,
These apt for richer soils, for lighter those:
Psithian for raisin-wine more useful, thin
Lageos, that one day will try the feet
And tie the tongue: purples and early-ripes,
And how, O Rhaetian, shall I hymn thy praise?
Yet cope not therefore with Falernian bins.
Vines Aminaean too, best-bodied wine,
To which the Tmolian bows him, ay, and king
Phanaeus too, and, lesser of that name,
Argitis, wherewith not a grape can vie
For gush of wine-juice or for length of years.
Nor thee must I pass over, vine of Rhodes,
Welcomed by gods and at the second board,
Nor thee, Bumastus, with plump clusters swollen.
But lo! how many kinds, and what their names,
There is no telling, nor doth it boot to tell;
Who lists to know it, he too would list to learn
How many sand-grains are by Zephyr tossed
On Libya's plain, or wot, when Eurus falls
With fury on the ships, how many waves
Come rolling shoreward from the Ionian sea.
    Not that all soils can all things bear alike.
Willows by water-courses have their birth,
Alders in miry fens; on rocky heights
The barren mountain-ashes; on the shore
Myrtles throng gayest; Bacchus, lastly, loves
The bare hillside, and yews the north wind's chill.
Mark too the earth by outland tillers tamed,
And Eastern homes of Arabs, and tattooed
Geloni; to all trees their native lands
Allotted are; no clime but India bears
Black ebony; the branch of frankincense
Is Saba's sons' alone; why tell to thee
Of balsams oozing from the perfumed wood,
Or berries of acanthus ever green?
Of Aethiop forests hoar with downy wool,
Or how the Seres comb from off the leaves

Their silky fleece? Of groves which India bears,
Ocean's near neighbour, earth's remotest nook,
Where not an arrow-shot can cleave the air
Above their tree-tops? yet no laggards they,
When girded with the quiver! Media yields
The bitter juices and slow-lingering taste
Of the blest citron-fruit, than which no aid
Comes timelier, when fierce step-dames drug the cup
With simples mixed and spells of baneful power,
To drive the deadly poison from the limbs.
Large the tree's self in semblance like a bay,
And, showered it not a different scent abroad,
A bay it had been; for no wind of heaven
Its foliage falls; the flower, none faster, clings;
With it the Medes for sweetness lave the lips,
And ease the panting breathlessness of age.

   But no, not Mede-land with its wealth of woods,
Nor Ganges fair, and Hermus thick with gold,
Can match the praise of Italy; nor Ind,
Nor Bactria, nor Panchaia, one wide tract
Of incense-teeming sand. Here never bulls
With nostrils snorting fire upturned the sod
Sown with the monstrous dragon's teeth, nor crop
Of warriors bristled thick with lance and helm;
But heavy harvests and the Massic juice
Of Bacchus fill its borders, overspread
With fruitful flocks and olives. Hence arose
The war-horse stepping proudly o'er the plain;
Hence thy white flocks, Clitumnus, and the bull,
Of victims mightiest, which full oft have led,
Bathed in thy sacred stream, the triumph-pomp
Of Romans to the temples of the gods.
Here blooms perpetual spring, and summer here
In months that are not summer's; twice teem the flocks;
Twice doth the tree yield service of her fruit.
But ravening tigers come not nigh, nor breed
Of savage lion, nor aconite betrays
Its hapless gatherers, nor with sweep so vast
Doth the scaled serpent trail his endless coils
Along the ground, or wreathe him into spires.
Mark too her cities, so many and so proud,
Of mighty toil the achievement, town on town
Up rugged precipices heaved and reared,

And rivers undergliding ancient walls.
Or should I celebrate the sea that laves
Her upper shores and lower? or those broad lakes?
Thee, Larius, greatest and, Benacus, thee
With billowy uproar surging like the main?
Or sing her harbours, and the barrier cast
Athwart the Lucrine, and how ocean chafes
With mighty bellowings, where the Julian wave
Echoes the thunder of his rout, and through
Avernian inlets pours the Tuscan tide?
A land no less that in her veins displays
Rivers of silver, mines of copper ore,
Ay, and with gold hath flowed abundantly.
A land that reared a valiant breed of men,
The Marsi and Sabellian youth, and, schooled
To hardship, the Ligurian, and with these
The Volscian javelin-armed, the Decii too,
The Marii and Camilli, names of might,
The Scipios, stubborn warriors, ay, and thee,
Great Caesar, who in Asia's utmost bounds
With conquering arm e'en now art fending far
The unwarlike Indian from the heights of Rome.
Hail! land of Saturn, mighty mother thou
Of fruits and heroes; 'tis for thee I dare
Unseal the sacred fountains, and essay
Themes of old art and glory, as I sing
The song of Ascra through the towns of Rome.
  Now for the native gifts of various soils,
What powers hath each, what hue, what natural bent
For yielding increase. First your stubborn lands
And churlish hill-sides, where are thorny fields
Of meagre marl and gravel, these delight
In long-lived olive-groves to Pallas dear.
Take for a sign the plenteous growth hard by
Of oleaster, and the fields strewn wide
With woodland berries. But a soil that's rich,
In moisture sweet exulting, and the plain
That teems with grasses on its fruitful breast,
Such as full oft in hollow mountain-dell
We view beneath us—from the craggy heights
Streams thither flow with fertilizing mud—
A plain which southward rising feeds the fern
By curvèd ploughs detested, this one day

Shall yield thee store of vines full strong to gush
In torrents of the wine-god; this shall be
Fruitful of grapes and flowing juice like that
We pour to heaven from bowls of gold, what time
The sleek Etruscan at the altar blows
His ivory pipe, and on the curvèd dish
We lay the reeking entrails. If to rear
Cattle delight thee rather, steers, or lambs,
Or goats that kill the tender plants, then seek
Full-fed Tarentum's glades and distant fields,
Or such a plain as luckless Mantua lost,
Whose weedy water feeds the snow-white swan:
There nor clear springs nor grass the flocks will fail,
And all the day-long browsing of thy herds
Shall the cool dews of one brief night repair.
Land which the burrowing share shows dark and rich,
With crumbling soil—for this we counterfeit
In ploughing—for corn is goodliest; from no field
More wains thou'lt see wend home with plodding steers;
Or that from which the husbandman in spleen
Has cleared the timber, and o'erthrown the copse
That year on year lay idle, and from the roots
Uptorn the immemorial haunt of birds;
They banished from their nests have sought the skies;
But the rude plain beneath the ploughshare's stroke
Starts into sudden brightness. For indeed
The starved hill-country gravel scarce serves the bees
With lowly cassias and with rosemary;
Rough tufa and chalk too, by black water-worms
Gnawed through and through, proclaim no soils beside
So rife with serpent-dainties, or that yield
Such winding lairs to lurk in. That again,
Which vapoury mist and flitting smoke exhales,
Drinks moisture up and casts it forth at will,
Which, ever in its own green grass arrayed,
Mars not the metal with salt scurf of rust—
That shall thine elms with merry vines enwreathe;
That teems with olive; that shall thy tilth prove kind
To cattle, and patient of the curvèd share.
Such ploughs rich Capua, such the coast that skirts
Thy ridge, Vesuvius, and the Clanian flood,
Acerrae's desolation and her bane.
How each to recognize now hear me tell.

Dost ask if loose or passing firm it be—
Since one for corn hath liking, one for wine,
The firmer sort for Ceres, none too loose
For thee, Lyaeus?—with scrutinizing eye
First choose thy ground, and bid a pit be sunk
Deep in the solid earth, then cast the mould
All back again, and stamp the surface smooth.
If it suffice not, loose will be the land,
More meet for cattle and for kindly vines;
But if, rebellious, to its proper bounds
The soil returns not, but fills all the trench
And overtops it, then the glebe is gross;
Look for stiff ridges and reluctant clods,
And with strong bullocks cleave the fallow crust.
Salt ground again, and bitter, as 'tis called—
Barren for fruits, by tilth untamable,
Nor grape her kind, nor apples their good name
Maintaining—will in this wise yield thee proof:
Stout osier-baskets from the rafter-smoke,
And strainers of the winepress pluck thee down;
Hereinto let that evil land, with fresh
Spring-water mixed, be trampled to the full;
The moisture, mark you, will ooze all away,
In big drops issuing through the osier-withes,
But plainly will its taste the secret tell,
And with a harsh twang ruefully distort
The mouths of them that try it. Rich soil again
We learn on this wise: tossed from hand to hand
Yet cracks it never, but pitch-like, as we hold,
Clings to the fingers. A land with moisture rife
Breeds lustier herbage, and is more than meet
Prolific. Ah! may never such for me
O'er-fertile prove, or make too stout a show
At the first earing! Heavy land or light
The mute self-witness of its weight betrays.
A glance will serve to warn thee which is black,
Or what the hue of any. But hard it is
To track the signs of that pernicious cold:
Pines only, noxious yews, and ivies dark
At times reveal its traces.
                              All these rules
Regarding, let your land, ay, long before,
Scorch to the quick, and into trenches carve

The mighty mountains, and their upturned clods
Bare to the north wind, ere thou plant therein
The vine's prolific kindred. Fields whose soil
Is crumbling are the best: winds look to that,
And bitter hoar-frosts, and the delver's toil
Untiring, as he stirs the loosened glebe.
But those, whose vigilance no care escapes,
Search for a kindred site, where first to rear
A nursery for the trees, and eke whereto
Soon to translate them, lest the sudden shock
From their new mother the young plants estrange.
Nay, even the quarter of the sky they brand
Upon the bark, that each may be restored,
As erst it stood, here bore the southern heats,
Here turned its shoulder to the northern pole;
So strong is custom formed in early years.
Whether on hill or plain 'tis best to plant
Your vineyard first inquire. If on some plain
You measure out rich acres, then plant thick;
Thick planting makes no niggard of the vine;
But if on rising mound or sloping hill,
Then let the rows have room, so none the less
Each line you draw, when all the trees are set,
May tally to perfection. Even as oft
In mighty war, whenas the legion's length
Deploys its cohorts, and the column stands
In open plain, the ranks of battle set,
And far and near with rippling sheen of arms
The wide earth flickers, nor yet in grisly strife
Foe grapples foe, but dubious 'twixt the hosts
The war-god wavers; so let all be ranged
In equal rows symmetric, not alone
To feed an idle fancy with the view,
But since not otherwise will earth afford
Vigour to all alike, nor yet the boughs
Have power to stretch them into open space.
   Shouldst haply of the furrow's depth inquire,
Even to a shallow trench I dare commit
The vine; but deeper in the ground is fixed
The tree that props it, aesculus in chief,
Which howso far its summit soars toward heaven,
So deep strikes root into the vaults of hell.
It therefore neither storms, nor blasts, nor showers

Wrench from its bed; unshaken it abides,
Sees many a generation, many an age
Of men roll onward, and survives them all,
Stretching its titan arms and branches far,
Sole central pillar of a world of shade.

    Nor toward the sunset let thy vineyards slope,
Nor midst the vines plant hazel; neither take
The topmost shoots for cuttings, nor from the top
Of the supporting tree your suckers tear;
So deep their love of earth; nor wound the plants
With blunted blade; nor truncheons intersperse
Of the wild olive: for oft from careless swains
A spark hath fallen, that, 'neath the unctuous rind
Hid thief-like first, now grips the tough tree-bole,
And mounting to the leaves on high, sends forth
A roar to heaven, then coursing through the boughs
And airy summits reigns victoriously,
Wraps all the grove in robes of fire, and gross
With pitch-black vapour heaves the murky reek
Skyward, but chiefly if a storm has swooped
Down on the forest, and a driving wind
Rolls up the conflagration. When 'tis so,
Their root-force fails them, nor, when lopped away,
Can they recover, and from the earth beneath
Spring to like verdure; thus alone survives
The bare wild olive with its bitter leaves.

    Let none persuade thee, howso weighty-wise,
To stir the soil when stiff with Boreas' breath.
Then ice-bound winter locks the fields, nor lets
The young plant fix its frozen root to earth.
Best sow your vineyards when in blushing Spring
Comes the white bird long-bodied snakes abhor,
Or on the eve of autumn's earliest frost,
Ere the swift sun-steeds touch the wintry Signs,
While summer is departing. Spring it is
Blesses the fruit-plantation, Spring the groves;
In Spring earth swells and claims the fruitful seed.
Then Aether, sire omnipotent, leaps down
With quickening showers to his glad wife's embrace,
And, might with might commingling, rears to life
All germs that teem within her; then resound
With songs of birds the greenwood-wildernesses,
And in due time the herds their loves renew;

Then the boon earth yields increase, and the fields
Unlock their bosoms to the warm west winds;
Soft moisture spreads o'er all things, and the blades
Face the new suns, and safely trust them now;
The vine-shoot, fearless of the rising south,
Or mighty north winds driving rain from heaven,
Bursts into bud, and every leaf unfolds.
Even so, methinks, when Earth to being sprang,
Dawned the first days, and such the course they held;
'Twas Spring-tide then, ay, Spring, the mighty world
Was keeping: Eurus spared his wintry blasts,
When first the flocks drank sunlight, and a race
Of men like iron from the hard glebe arose,
And wild beasts thronged the woods, and stars the heaven.
Nor could frail creatures bear this heavy strain,
Did not so large a respite interpose
'Twixt frost and heat, and heaven's relenting arms
Yield earth a welcome.
                              For the rest, whate'er
The sets thou plantest in thy fields, thereon
Strew refuse rich, and with abundant earth
Take heed to hide them, and dig in withal
Rough shells or porous stone, for therebetween
Will water trickle and fine vapour creep,
And so the plants their drooping spirits raise.
Aye, and there have been, who with weight of stone
Or heavy potsherd press them from above;
This serves for shield in pelting showers, and this
When the hot dog-star chaps the fields with drought.
   The slips once planted, yet remains to cleave
The earth about their roots persistently,
And toss the cumbrous hoes, or task the soil
With burrowing plough-share, and ply up and down
Your labouring bullocks through the vineyard's midst,
Then too smooth reeds and shafts of whittled wand,
And ashen poles and sturdy forks to shape,
Whereby supported they may learn to mount,
Laugh at the gales, and through the elm-tops win
From story up to story.
                              Now while yet
The leaves are in their first fresh infant growth,
Forbear their frailty, and while yet the bough
Shoots joyfully toward heaven, with loosened rein

Launched on the void, assail it not as yet
With keen-edged sickle, but let the leaves alone
Be culled with clip of fingers here and there.
But when they clasp the elms with sturdy trunks
Erect, then strip the leaves off, prune the boughs;
Sooner they shrink from steel, but then put forth
The arm of power, and stem the branchy tide.

　　Hedges too must be woven and all beasts
Barred entrance, chiefly while the leaf is young
And witless of disaster; for therewith,
Beside harsh winters and o'erpowering sun,
Wild buffaloes and pestering goats for ay
Besport them, sheep and heifers glut their greed.
Nor cold by hoar-frost curdled, nor the prone
Dead weight of summer upon the parchèd crags,
So scathe it, as the flocks with venom-bite
Of their hard tooth, whose gnawing scars the stem.
For no offence but this to Bacchus bleeds
The goat at every altar, and old plays
Upon the stage find entrance; therefore too
The sons of Theseus through the country-side—
Hamlet and crossway—set the prize of wit,
And on the smooth sward over oilèd skins
Dance in their tipsy frolic. Furthermore
The Ausonian swains, a race from Troy derived,
Make merry with rough rhymes and boisterous mirth,
Grim masks of hollowed bark assume, invoke
Thee with glad hymns, O Bacchus, and to thee
Hang puppet-faces on tall pines to swing.
Hence every vineyard teems with mellowing fruit,
Till hollow vale o'erflows, and gorge profound,
Where'er the god hath turned his comely head.
Therefore to Bacchus duly will we sing
Meet honour with ancestral hymns, and cates
And dishes bear him; and the doomèd goat
Led by the horn shall at the altar stand,
Whose entrails rich on hazel-spits we'll roast.

　　This further task again, to dress the vine,
Hath needs beyond exhausting; the whole soil
Thrice, four times, yearly must be cleft, the sod
With hoes reversed be crushed continually,
The whole plantation lightened of its leaves.
Round on the labourer spins the wheel of toil,

As on its own track rolls the circling year.
Soon as the vine her lingering leaves hath shed,
And the chill north wind from the forests shook
Their coronal, even then the careful swain
Looks keenly forward to the coming year,
With Saturn's curvèd fang pursues and prunes
The vine forlorn, and lops it into shape.
Be first to dig the ground up, first to clear
And burn the refuse-branches, first to house
Again your vine-poles, last to gather fruit.
Twice doth the thickening shade beset the vine,
Twice weeds with stifling briers o'ergrow the crop;
And each a toilsome labour. Do thou praise
Broad acres, farm but few. Rough twigs beside
Of butcher's broom among the woods are cut,
And reeds upon the river-banks, and still
The undressed willow claims thy fostering care.
So now the vines are fettered, now the trees
Let go the sickle, and the last dresser now
Sings of his finished rows; but still the ground
Must vexèd be, the dust be stirred, and heaven
Still set thee trembling for the ripened grapes.

Not so with olives; small husbandry need they,
Nor look for sickle bowed or biting rake,
When once they have gripped the soil, and borne the breeze.
Earth of herself, with hookèd fang laid bare,
Yields moisture for the plants, and heavy fruit,
The ploughshare aiding; therewithal thou'lt rear
The olive's fatness well-beloved of Peace.

Apples, moreover, soon as first they feel
Their stems wax lusty, and have found their strength,
To heaven climb swiftly, self-impelled, nor crave
Our succour. All the grove meanwhile no less
With fruit is swelling, and the wild haunts of birds
Blush with their blood-red berries. Cytisus
Is good to browse on, the tall forest yields
Pine-torches, and the nightly fires are fed
And shoot forth radiance. And shall men be loath
To plant, nor lavish of their pains? Why trace
Things mightier? Willows even and lowly brooms
To cattle their green leaves, to shepherds shade,
Fences for crops, and food for honey yield.
And blithe it is Cytorus to behold

Waving with box, Narycian groves of pitch;
Oh! blithe the sight of fields beholden not
To rake or man's endeavour! the barren woods
That crown the scalp of Caucasus, even these,
Which furious blasts for ever rive and rend,
Yield various wealth, pine-logs that serve for ships,
Cedar and cypress for the homes of men;
Hence, too, the farmers shave their wheel-spokes, hence
Drums for their wains, and curvèd boat-keels fit;
Willows bear twigs enow, the elm-tree leaves,
Myrtle stout spear-shafts, war-tried cornel too;
Yews into Ituraean bows are bent:
Nor do smooth lindens or lathe-polished box
Shrink from man's shaping and keen-furrowing steel;
Light alder floats upon the boiling flood
Sped down the Padus, and bees house their swarms
In rotten holm-oak's hollow bark and bole.
What of like praise can Bacchus' gifts afford?
Nay, Bacchus even to crime hath prompted, he
The wine-infuriate Centaurs quelled with death,
Rhoetus and Pholus, and with mighty bowl
Hylaeus threatening high the Lapithae.
   Oh! all too happy tillers of the soil,
Could they but know their blessedness, for whom
Far from the clash of arms all-equal earth
Pours from the ground herself their easy fare!
What though no lofty palace portal-proud
From all its chambers vomits forth a tide
Of morning courtiers, nor agape they gaze
On pillars with fair tortoise-shell inwrought,
Gold-purfled robes, and bronze from Ephyre;
Nor is the whiteness of their wool distained
With drugs Assyrian, nor clear olive's use
With cassia tainted; yet untroubled calm,
A life that knows no falsehood, rich enow
With various treasures, yet broad-acred ease,
Grottoes and living lakes, yet Tempes cool,
Lowing of kine, and sylvan slumbers soft,
They lack not; lawns and wild beasts' haunts are there,
A youth of labour patient, need-inured,
Worship, and reverend sires: with them from earth
Departing justice her last footprints left.
   Me before all things may the Muses sweet,

Whose rites I bear with mighty passion pierced,
Receive, and show the paths and stars of heaven,
The sun's eclipses and the labouring moons,
From whence the earthquake, by what power the seas
Swell from their depths, and, every barrier burst,
Sink back upon themselves, why winter-suns
So haste to dip 'neath ocean, or what check
The lingering night retards. But if to these
High realms of nature the cold curdling blood
About my heart bar access, then be fields
And stream-washed vales my solace, let me love
Rivers and woods, inglorious. Oh for you
Plains, and Spercheius, and Taygete,
By Spartan maids o'er-revelled! Oh, for one,
Would set me in deep dells of Haemus cool,
And shield me with his boughs' o'ershadowing might!
Happy, who had the skill to understand
Nature's hid causes, and beneath his feet
All terrors cast, and death's relentless doom,
And the loud roar of greedy Acheron.
Blest too is he who knows the rural gods,
Pan, old Silvanus, and the sister-nymphs!
Him nor the rods of public power can bend,
Nor kingly purple, nor fierce feud that drives
Brother to turn on brother, nor descent
Of Dacian from the Danube's leaguèd flood,
Nor Rome's great State, nor kingdoms like to die;
Nor hath he grieved through pitying of the poor,
Nor envied him that hath. What fruit the boughs,
And what the fields, of their own bounteous will
Have borne, he gathers; nor iron rule of laws,
Nor maddened Forum have his eyes beheld,
Nor archives of the people. Others vex
The darksome gulfs of Ocean with their oars,
Or rush on steel: they press within the courts
And doors of princes; one with havoc falls
Upon a city and its hapless hearths,
From gems to drink, on Tyrian rugs to lie;
This hoards his wealth and broods o'er buried gold;
One at the rostra stares in blank amaze;
One gaping sits transported by the cheers,
The answering cheers of plebs and senate rolled
Along the benches: bathed in brothers' blood

Men revel, and, all delights of hearth and home
For exile changing, a new country seek
Beneath an alien sun. The husbandman
With hookèd ploughshare turns the soil; from hence
Springs his year's labour; hence, too, he sustains
Country and cottage homestead, and from hence
His herds of cattle and deserving steers.
No respite! still the year o'erflows with fruit,
Or young of kine, or Ceres' wheaten sheaf,
With crops the furrow loads, and bursts the barns.
Winter is come: in olive-mills they bruise
The Sicyonian berry; acorn-cheered
The swine troop homeward; woods their arbutes yield;
So, various fruit sheds Autumn, and high up
On sunny rocks the mellowing vintage bakes.
Meanwhile about his lips sweet children cling;
His chaste house keeps its purity; his kine
Drop milky udders, and on the lush green grass
Fat kids are striving, horn to butting horn.
Himself keeps holy days; stretched o'er the sward,
Where round the fire his comrades crown the bowl,
He pours libation, and thy name invokes,
Lenaeus, and for the herdsmen on an elm
Sets up a mark for the swift javelin; they
Strip their tough bodies for the rustic sport.
Such life of yore the ancient Sabines led,
Such Remus and his brother: Etruria thus,
Doubt not, to greatness grew, and Rome became
The fair world's fairest, and with circling wall
Clasped to her single breast the sevenfold hills.
Ay, ere the reign of Dicte's king, ere men,
Waxed godless, banqueted on slaughtered bulls,
Such life on earth did golden Saturn lead.
Nor ear of man had heard the war-trump's blast,
Nor clang of sword on stubborn anvil set.
     But lo! a boundless space we have travelled o'er;
'Tis time our steaming horses to unyoke.

# GEORGIC III

Thee too, great Pales, will I hymn, and thee,
Amphrysian shepherd, worthy to be sung,
You, woods and waves Lycaean. All themes beside,
Which else had charmed the vacant mind with song,
Are now waxed common. Of harsh Eurystheus who
The story knows not, or that praiseless king
Busiris, and his altars? or by whom
Hath not the tale been told of Hylas young,
Latonian Delos and Hippodame,
And Pelops for his ivory shoulder famed,
Keen charioteer? Needs must a path be tried,
By which I too may lift me from the dust,
And float triumphant through the mouths of men.
Yea, I shall be the first, so life endure,
To lead the Muses with me, as I pass
To mine own country from the Aonian height;
I, Mantua, first will bring thee back the palms
Of Idumaea, and raise a marble shrine
On thy green plain fast by the water-side,
Where Mincius winds more vast in lazy coils,
And rims his margent with the tender reed.
Amid my shrine shall Caesar's godhead dwell.
To him will I, as victor, bravely dight
In Tyrian purple, drive along the bank
A hundred four-horse cars. All Greece for me,
Leaving Alpheus and Molorchus' grove,
On foot shall strive, or with the raw-hide glove;
Whilst I, my head with stripped green olive crowned,
Will offer gifts. Even now 'tis present joy
To lead the high processions to the fane,
And view the victims felled; or how the scene

Sunders with shifted face, and Britain's sons
Inwoven thereon with those proud curtains rise.
Of gold and massive ivory on the doors
I'll trace the battle of the Gangarides,
And our Quirinus' conquering arms, and there
Surging with war, and hugely flowing, the Nile,
And columns heaped on high with naval brass.
And Asia's vanquished cities I will add,
And quelled Niphates, and the Parthian foe,
Who trusts in flight and backward-volleying darts,
And trophies torn with twice triumphant hand
From empires twain on ocean's either shore.
And breathing forms of Parian marble there
Shall stand, the offspring of Assaracus,
And great names of the Jove-descended folk,
And father Tros, and Troy's first founder, lord
Of Cynthus. And accursèd Envy there
Shall dread the Furies, and thy ruthless flood,
Cocytus, and Ixion's twisted snakes,
And that vast wheel and ever-baffling stone.
Meanwhile the Dryad-haunted woods and lawns
Unsullied seek we; 'tis thy hard behest,
Maecenas. Without thee no lofty task
My mind essays. Up! break the sluggish bonds
Of tarriance; with loud din Cithaeron calls,
Steed-taming Epidaurus, and thy hounds,
Taygete; and hark! the assenting groves
With peal on peal reverberate the roar.
Yet must I gird me to rehearse ere long
The fiery fights of Caesar, speed his name
Through ages, countless as to Caesar's self
From the first birth-dawn of Tithonus old.
  If eager for the prized Olympian palm
One breed the horse, or bullock strong to plough,
Be his prime care a shapely dam to choose.
Of kine grim-faced is goodliest, with coarse head
And burly neck, whose hanging dewlaps reach
From chin to knee; of boundless length her flank;
Large every way she is, large-footed even,
With incurved horns and shaggy ears beneath.
Nor let mislike me one with spots of white
Conspicuous, or that spurns the yoke, whose horn
At times hath vice in't: liker bull-faced she,

And tall-limbed wholly, and with tip of tail
Brushing her footsteps as she walks along.
The age for Hymen's rites, Lucina's pangs,
Ere ten years ended, after four begins;
Their residue of days nor apt to teem,
Nor strong for ploughing. Meantime, while youth's delight
Survives within them, loose the males: be first
To speed thy herds of cattle to their loves,
Breed stock with stock, and keep the race supplied.
Ah! life's best hours are ever first to fly
From hapless mortals; in their place succeed
Disease and dolorous eld; till travail sore
And death unpitying sweep them from the scene.
Still will be some, whose form thou fain wouldst change;
Renew them still; with yearly choice of young
Preventing losses, lest too late thou rue.

 Nor steeds crave less selection; but on those
Thou think'st to rear, the promise of their line,
From earliest youth thy chiefest pains bestow.
See from the first yon high-bred colt afield,
His lofty step, his limbs' elastic tread:
Dauntless he leads the herd, still first to try
The threatening flood, or brave the unknown bridge,
By no vain noise affrighted; lofty-necked,
With clean-cut head, short belly, and stout back;
His sprightly breast exuberant with brawn.
Chestnut and grey are good; the worst-hued white
And sorrel. Then lo! if arms are clashed afar,
Bide still he cannot: ears stiffen and limbs quake;
His nostrils snort and roll out wreaths of fire.
Dense is his mane, that when uplifted falls
On his right shoulder; betwixt either loin
The spine runs double; his earth-dinting hoof
Rings with the ponderous beat of solid horn.
Even such a horse was Cyllarus, reined and tamed
By Pollux of Amyclae; such the pair
In Grecian song renowned, those steeds of Mars,
And famed Achilles' team: in such-like form
Great Saturn's self with mane flung loose on neck
Sped at his wife's approach, and flying filled
The heights of Pelion with his piercing neigh.

 Even him, when sore disease or sluggish eld
Now saps his strength, pen fast at home, and spare

His not inglorious age. A horse grown old
Slow kindling unto love in vain prolongs
The fruitless task, and, to the encounter come,
As fire in stubble blusters without strength,
He rages idly. Therefore mark thou first
Their age and mettle, other points anon,
As breed and lineage, or what pain was theirs
To lose the race, what pride the palm to win.
Seest how the chariots in mad rivalry
Poured from the barrier grip the course and go,
When youthful hope is highest, and every heart
Drained with each wild pulsation? How they ply
The circling lash, and reaching forward let
The reins hang free! Swift spins the glowing wheel;
And now they stoop, and now erect in air
Seem borne through space and towering to the sky:
No stop, no stay; the dun sand whirls aloft;
They reek with foam-flakes and pursuing breath;
So sweet is fame, so prized the victor's palm.
'Twas Ericthonius first took heart to yoke
Four horses to his car, and rode above
The whirling wheels to victory: but the ring
And bridle-reins, mounted on horses' backs,
The Pelethronian Lapithae bequeathed,
And taught the knight in arms to spurn the ground,
And arch the upgathered footsteps of his pride.
Each task alike is arduous, and for each
A horse young, fiery, swift of foot, they seek;
How oft so-e'er yon rival may have chased
The flying foe, or boast his native plain
Epirus, or Mycenae's stubborn hold,
And trace his lineage back to Neptune's birth.
    These points regarded, as the time draws nigh,
With instant zeal they lavish all their care
To plump with solid fat the chosen chief
And designated husband of the herd:
And flowery herbs they cut, and serve him well
With corn and running water, that his strength
Not fail him for that labour of delight,
Nor puny colts betray the feeble sire.
The herd itself of purpose they reduce
To leanness, and when love's sweet longing first
Provokes them, they forbid the leafy food,

And pen them from the springs, and oft beside
With running shake, and tire them in the sun,
What time the threshing-floor groans heavily
With pounding of the corn-ears, and light chaff
Is whirled on high to catch the rising west.
This do they that the soil's prolific powers
May not be dulled by surfeiting, nor choke
The sluggish furrows, but eagerly absorb
Their fill of love, and deeply entertain.
　　To care of sire the mother's care succeeds.
When great with young they wander nigh their time,
Let no man suffer them to drag the yoke
In heavy wains, nor leap across the way,
Nor scour the meads, nor swim the rushing flood.
In lonely lawns they feed them, by the course
Of brimming streams, where moss is, and the banks
With grass are greenest, where are sheltering caves,
And far outstretched the rock-flung shadow lies.
Round wooded Silarus and the ilex-bowers
Of green Alburnus swarms a wingèd pest—
Its Roman name Asilus, by the Greeks
Termed Oestros—fierce it is, and harshly hums,
Driving whole herds in terror through the groves,
Till heaven is madded by their bellowing din,
And Tanager's dry bed and forest-banks.
With this same scourge did Juno wreak of old
The terrors of her wrath, a plague devised
Against the heifer sprung from Inachus.
From this too thou, since in the noontide heats
'Tis most persistent, fend thy teeming herds,
And feed them when the sun is newly risen,
Or the first stars are ushering in the night.
　　But, yeaning ended, all their tender care
Is to the calves transferred; at once with marks
They brand them, both to designate their race,
And which to rear for breeding, or devote
As altar-victims, or to cleave the ground
And into ridges tear and turn the sod.
The rest along the greensward graze at will.
Those that to rustic uses thou wouldst mould,
As calves encourage and take steps to tame,
While pliant wills and plastic youth allow.
And first of slender withies round the throat

Loose collars hang, then when their free-born necks
Are used to service, with the self-same bands
Yoke them in pairs, and steer by steer compel
Keep pace together. And time it is that oft
Unfreighted wheels be drawn along the ground
Behind them, as to dint the surface-dust;
Then let the beechen axle strain and creak
'Neath some stout burden, whilst a brazen pole
Drags on the wheels made fast thereto. Meanwhile
For their unbroken youth not grass alone,
Nor meagre willow-leaves and marish-sedge,
But corn-ears with thy hand pluck from the crops.
Nor shall the brood-kine, as of yore, for thee
Brim high the snowy milking-pail, but spend
Their udders' fullness on their own sweet young.

But if fierce squadrons and the ranks of war
Delight thee rather, or on wheels to glide
At Pisa, with Alpheus fleeting by,
And in the grove of Jupiter urge on
The flying chariot, be your steed's first task
To face the warrior's armèd rage, and brook
The trumpet, and long roar of rumbling wheels,
And clink of chiming bridles in the stall;
Then more and more to love his master's voice
Caressing, or loud hand that claps his neck.
Ay, thus far let him learn to dare, when first
Weaned from his mother, and his mouth at times
Yield to the supple halter, even while yet
Weak, tottering-limbed, and ignorant of life.
But, three years ended, when the fourth arrives,
Now let him tarry not to run the ring
With rhythmic hoof-beat echoing, and now learn
Alternately to curve each bending leg,
And be like one that struggleth; then at last
Challenge the winds to race him, and at speed
Launched through the open, like a reinless thing,
Scarce print his footsteps on the surface-sand.
As when with power from Hyperborean climes
The north wind stoops, and scatters from his path
Dry clouds and storms of Scythia; the tall corn
And rippling plains 'gin shiver with light gusts;
A sound is heard among the forest-tops;
Long waves come racing shoreward: fast he flies,

With instant pinion sweeping earth and main.
   A steed like this or on the mighty course
Of Elis at the goal will sweat, and shower
Red foam-flakes from his mouth, or, kindlier task,
With patient neck support the Belgian car.
Then, broken at last, let swell their burly frame
With fattening corn-mash, for, unbroke, they will
With pride wax wanton, and, when caught, refuse
Tough lash to brook or jaggèd curb obey.
   But no device so fortifies their power
As love's blind stings of passion to forefend,
Whether on steed or steer thy choice be set.
Ay, therefore 'tis they banish bulls afar
To solitary pastures, or behind
Some mountain-barrier, or broad streams beyond,
Or else in plenteous stalls pen fast at home.
For, even through sight of her, the female wastes
His strength with smouldering fire, till he forget
Both grass and woodland. She indeed full oft
With her sweet charms can lovers proud compel
To battle for the conquest horn to horn.
In Sila's forest feeds the heifer fair,
While each on each the furious rivals run;
Wound follows wound; the black blood laves their limbs;
Horns push and strive against opposing horns,
With mighty groaning; all the forest-side
And far Olympus bellow back the roar.
Nor wont the champions in one stall to couch;
But he that's worsted hies him to strange climes
Far off, an exile, moaning much the shame,
The blows of that proud conqueror, then love's loss
Avenged not; with one glance toward the byre,
His ancient royalties behind him lie.
So with all heed his strength he practiseth,
And nightlong makes the hard bare stones his bed,
And feeds on prickly leaf and pointed rush,
And proves himself, and butting at a tree
Learns to fling wrath into his horns, with blows
Provokes the air, and scattering clouds of sand
Makes prelude of the battle; afterward,
With strength repaired and gathered might breaks camp,
And hurls him headlong on the unthinking foe:
As in mid ocean when a wave far off

Begins to whiten, mustering from the main
Its rounded breast, and, onward rolled to land
Falls with prodigious roar among the rocks,
Huge as a very mountain: but the depths
Upseethe in swirling eddies, and disgorge
The murky sand-lees from their sunken bed.
    Nay, every race on earth of men, and beasts,
And ocean-folk, and flocks, and painted birds,
Rush to the raging fire: love sways them all.
Never than then more fiercely o'er the plain
Prowls heedless of her whelps the lioness:
Nor monstrous bears such wide-spread havoc-doom
Deal through the forests; then the boar is fierce,
Most deadly then the tigress: then, alack!
Ill roaming is it on Libya's lonely plains.
Mark you what shivering thrills the horse's frame,
If but a waft the well-known gust conveys?
Nor curb can check them then, nor lash severe,
Nor rocks and caverned crags, nor barrier-floods,
That rend and whirl and wash the hills away.
Then speeds amain the great Sabellian boar,
His tushes whets, with forefoot tears the ground,
Rubs 'gainst a tree his flanks, and to and fro
Hardens each wallowing shoulder to the wound.
What of the youth, when love's relentless might
Stirs the fierce fire within his veins? Behold!
In blindest midnight how he swims the gulf
Convulsed with bursting storm-clouds! Over him
Heaven's huge gate thunders; the rock-shattered main
Utters a warning cry; nor parents' tears
Can backward call him, nor the maid he loves,
Too soon to die on his untimely pyre.
What of the spotted ounce to Bacchus dear,
Or warlike wolf-kin or the breed of dogs?
Why tell how timorous stags the battle join?
O'er all conspicuous is the rage of mares,
By Venus' self inspired of old, what time
The Potnian four with rending jaws devoured
The limbs of Glaucus. Love-constrained they roam
Past Gargarus, past the loud Ascanian flood;
They climb the mountains, and the torrents swim;
And when their eager marrow first conceives
The fire, in Spring-tide chiefly, for with Spring

Warmth doth their frames revisit, then they stand
All facing westward on the rocky heights,
And of the gentle breezes take their fill;
And oft unmated, marvellous to tell,
But of the wind impregnate, far and wide
O'er craggy height and lowly vale they scud,
Not toward thy rising, Eurus, or the sun's,
But westward and north-west, or whence up-springs
Black Auster, that glooms heaven with rainy cold.
Hence from their groin slow drips a poisonous juice,
By shepherds truly named hippomanes,
Hippomanes, fell stepdames oft have culled,
And mixed with herbs and spells of baneful bode.
    Fast flies meanwhile the irreparable hour,
As point to point our charmèd round we trace.
Enough of herds. This second task remains,
The wool-clad flocks and shaggy goats to treat.
Here lies a labour; hence for glory look,
Brave husbandmen. Nor doubtfully know I
How hard it is for words to triumph here,
And shed their lustre on a theme so slight:
But I am caught by ravishing desire
Above the lone Parnassian steep; I love
To walk the heights, from whence no earlier track
Slopes gently downward to Castalia's spring.
    Now, awful Pales, strike a louder tone.
First, for the sheep soft pencotes I decree
To browse in, till green summer's swift return;
And that the hard earth under them with straw
And handfuls of the fern be littered deep,
Lest chill of ice such tender cattle harm
With scab and loathly foot-rot. Passing thence
I bid the goats with arbute-leaves be stored,
And served with fresh spring-water, and their pens
Turned southward from the blast, to face the suns
Of winter, when Aquarius' icy beam
Now sinks in showers upon the parting year.
These too no lightlier our protection claim,
Nor prove of poorer service, howsoe'er
Milesian fleeces dipped in Tyrian reds
Repay the barterer; these with offspring teem
More numerous; these yield plenteous store of milk:
The more each dry-wrung udder froths the pail,

More copious soon the teat-pressed torrents flow.
Ay, and on Cinyps' bank the he-goats too
Their beards and grizzled chins and bristling hair
Let clip for camp-use, or as rugs to wrap
Seafaring wretches. But they browse the woods
And summits of Lycaeus, and rough briers,
And brakes that love the highland: of themselves
Right heedfully the she-goats homeward troop
Before their kids, and with plump udders clogged
Scarce cross the threshold. Wherefore rather ye,
The less they crave man's vigilance, be fain
From ice to fend them and from snowy winds;
Bring food and feast them with their branchy fare,
Nor lock your hay-loft all the winter long.

   But when glad summer at the west wind's call
Sends either flock to pasture in the glades,
Soon as the day-star shineth, hie we then
To the cool meadows, while the dawn is young,
The grass yet hoary, and to browsing herds
The dew tastes sweetest on the tender sward.
When heaven's fourth hour draws on the thickening drought,
And shrill cicalas pierce the brake with song,
Then at the well-springs bid them, or deep pools,
From troughs of holm-oak quaff the running wave:
But at day's hottest seek a shadowy vale,
Where some vast ancient-timbered oak of Jove
Spreads his huge branches, or where huddling black
Ilex on ilex cowers in awful shade.
Then once more give them water sparingly,
And feed once more, till sunset, when cool eve
Allays the air, and dewy moonbeams slake
The forest glades, with halcyon's song the shore,
And every thicket with the goldfinch rings.
   Of Libya's shepherds why the tale pursue?
Why sing their pastures and the scattered huts
They house in? Oft their cattle day and night
Graze the whole month together, and go forth
Into far deserts where no shelter is,
So flat the plain and boundless. All his goods
The Afric swain bears with him, house and home,
Arms, Cretan quiver, and Amyclaean dog;
As some keen Roman in his country's arms
Plies the swift march beneath a cruel load;

Soon with tents pitched and at his post he stands,
Ere looked for by the foe. Not thus the tribes
Of Scythia by the far Maeotic wave,
Where turbid Ister whirls his yellow sands,
And Rhodope stretched out beneath the pole
Comes trending backward. There the herds they keep
Close-pent in byres, nor any grass is seen
Upon the plain, nor leaves upon the tree:
But with snow-ridges and deep frost afar
Heaped seven ells high the earth lies featureless:
Still winter! still the north wind's icy breath!
Nay, never sun disparts the shadows pale,
Or as he rides the steep of heaven, or dips
In ocean's fiery bath his plunging car.
Quick ice-crusts curdle on the running stream,
And iron-hooped wheels the water's back now bears,
To broad wains opened, as erewhile to ships;
Brass vessels oft asunder burst, and clothes
Stiffen upon the wearers; juicy wines
They cleave with axes; to one frozen mass
Whole pools are turned; and on their untrimmed beards
Stiff clings the jaggèd icicle. Meanwhile
All heaven no less is filled with falling snow;
The cattle perish: oxen's mighty frames
Stand island-like amid the frost, and stags
In huddling herds, by that strange weight benumbed,
Scarce top the surface with their antler-points.
These with no hounds they hunt, nor net with toils,
Nor scare with terror of the crimson plume;
But, as in vain they breast the opposing block,
Butcher them, knife in hand, and so dispatch
Loud-bellowing, and with glad shouts hale them home.
Themselves in deep-dug caverns underground
Dwell free and careless; to their hearths they heave
Oak-logs and elm-trees whole, and fire them there,
There play the night out, and in festive glee
With barm and service sour the wine-cup mock.
So 'neath the seven-starred Hyperborean wain
The folk live tameless, buffeted with blasts
Of Eurus from Rhipaean hills, and wrap
Their bodies in the tawny fells of beasts.

　　If wool delight thee, first, be far removed
All prickly boskage, burrs and caltrops; shun

Luxuriant pastures; at the outset choose
White flocks with downy fleeces. For the ram,
How white soe'er himself, be but the tongue
'Neath his moist palate black, reject him, lest
He sully with dark spots his offspring's fleece,
And seek some other o'er the teeming plain.
Even with such snowy bribe of wool, if ear
May trust the tale, Pan, God of Arcady,
Snared and beguiled thee, Luna, calling thee
To the deep woods; nor thou didst spurn his call.

　　But who for milk hath longing, must himself
Carry lucerne and lotus-leaves enow
With salt herbs to the cote, whence more they love
The streams, more stretch their udders, and give back
A subtle taste of saltness in the milk.
Many there be who from their mothers keep
The new-born kids, and straightway bind their mouths
With iron-tipped muzzles. What they milk at dawn,
Or in the daylight hours, at night they press;
What darkling or at sunset, this ere morn
They bear away in baskets—for to town
The shepherd hies him—or with dash of salt
Just sprinkle, and lay by for winter use.

　　Nor be thy dogs last cared for; but alike
Swift Spartan hounds and fierce Molossian feed
On fattening whey. Never, with these to watch,
Dread nightly thief afold and ravening wolves,
Or Spanish desperadoes in the rear.
And oft the shy wild asses thou wilt chase,
With hounds, too, hunt the hare, with hounds the doe;
Oft from his woodland wallowing-den uprouse
The boar, and scare him with their baying, and drive,
And o'er the mountains urge into the toils
Some antlered monster to their chiming cry.

　　Learn also scented cedar-wood to burn
Within the stalls, and snakes of noxious smell
With fumes of galbanum to drive away.
Oft under long-neglected cribs, or lurks
A viper ill to handle, that hath fled
The light in terror, or some snake, that wont
'Neath shade and sheltering roof to creep, and shower
Its bane among the cattle, hugs the ground,
Fell scourge of kine. Shepherd, seize stakes, seize stones!

And as he rears defiance, and puffs out
A hissing throat, down with him! see how low
That cowering crest is vailed in flight, the while,
His midmost coils and final sweep of tail
Relaxing, the last fold drags lingering spires.
Then that vile worm that in Calabrian glades
Uprears his breast, and wreathes a scaly back,
His length of belly pied with mighty spots—
While from their founts gush any streams, while yet
With showers of Spring and rainy south-winds earth
Is moistened, lo! he haunts the pools, and here
Housed in the banks, with fish and chattering frogs
Crams the black void of his insatiate maw.
Soon as the fens are parched, and earth with heat
Is gaping, forth he darts into the dry,
Rolls eyes of fire and rages through the fields,
Furious from thirst and by the drought dismayed.
Me list not then beneath the open heaven
To snatch soft slumber, nor on forest-ridge
Lie stretched along the grass, when, slipped his slough,
To glittering youth transformed he winds his spires,
And eggs or younglings leaving in his lair,
Towers sunward, lightening with three-forkèd tongue.
    Of sickness, too, the causes and the signs
I'll teach thee. Loathly scab assails the sheep,
When chilly showers have probed them to the quick,
And winter stark with hoar-frost, or when sweat
Unpurged cleaves to them after shearing done,
And rough thorns rend their bodies. Hence it is
Shepherds their whole flock steep in running streams,
While, plunged beneath the flood, with drenchèd fell,
The ram, launched free, goes drifting down the tide.
Else, having shorn, they smear their bodies o'er
With acrid oil-lees, and mix silver-scum
And native sulphur and Idaean pitch,
Wax mollified with ointment, and therewith
Sea-leek, strong hellebores, bitumen black.
Yet ne'er doth kindlier fortune crown his toil,
Than if with blade of iron a man dare lance
The ulcer's mouth ope: for the taint is fed
And quickened by confinement; while the swain
His hand of healing from the wound withholds,
Or sits for happier signs imploring heaven.

Aye, and when inward to the bleater's bones
The pain hath sunk and rages, and their limbs
By thirsty fever are consumed, 'tis good
To draw the enkindled heat therefrom, and pierce
Within the hoof-clefts a blood-bounding vein.
Of tribes Bisaltic such the wonted use,
And keen Gelonian, when to Rhodope
He flies, or Getic desert, and quaffs milk
With horse-blood curdled.
                          Seest one far afield
Oft to the shade's mild covert win, or pull
The grass tops listlessly, or hindmost lag,
Or, browsing, cast her down amid the plain,
At night retire belated and alone;
With quick knife check the mischief, ere it creep
With dire contagion through the unwary herd.
Less thick and fast the whirlwind scours the main
With tempest in its wake, than swarm the plagues
Of cattle; nor seize they single lives alone,
But sudden clear whole feeding grounds, the flock
With all its promise, and extirpate the breed.
Well would he trow it who, so long after, still
High Alps and Noric hill-forts should behold,
And Iapydian Timavus' fields,
Ay, still behold the shepherds' realms a waste,
And far and wide the lawns untenanted.

   Here from distempered heavens erewhile arose
A piteous season, with the full fierce heat
Of autumn glowed, and cattle-kindreds all
And all wild creatures to destruction gave,
Tainted the pools, the fodder charged with bane.
Nor simple was the way of death, but when
Hot thirst through every vein impelled had drawn
Their wretched limbs together, anon o'erflowed
A watery flux, and all their bones piecemeal
Sapped by corruption to itself absorbed.
Oft in mid sacrifice to heaven—the white
Wool-woven fillet half wreathed about his brow—
Some victim, standing by the altar, there
Betwixt the loitering carles a-dying fell:
Or, if betimes the slaughtering priest had struck,
Nor with its heapèd entrails blazed the pile,
Nor seer to seeker thence could answer yield;

Nay, scarce the up-stabbing knife with blood was stained,
Scarce sullied with thin gore the surface-sand.
Hence die the calves in many a pasture fair,
Or at full cribs their lives' sweet breath resign;
Hence on the fawning dog comes madness, hence
Racks the sick swine a gasping cough that chokes
With swelling at the jaws: the conquering steed,
Uncrowned of effort and heedless of the sward,
Faints, turns him from the springs, and paws the earth
With ceaseless hoof: low droop his ears, wherefrom
Bursts fitful sweat, a sweat that waxes cold
Upon the dying beast; the skin is dry,
And rigidly repels the handler's touch.
These earlier signs they give that presage doom.
But, if the advancing plague 'gin fiercer grow,
Then are their eyes all fire, deep-drawn their breath,
At times groan-laboured: with long sobbing heave
Their lowest flanks; from either nostril streams
Black blood; a rough tongue clogs the obstructed jaws.
'Twas helpful through inverted horn to pour
Draughts of the wine-god down; sole way it seemed
To save the dying: soon this too proved their bane,
And, reinvigorate but with frenzy's fire,
Even at death's pinch—the gods some happier fate
Deal to the just, such madness to their foes—
Each with bared teeth his own limbs mangling tore.
See! as he smokes beneath the stubborn share,
The bull drops, vomiting foam-dabbled gore,
And heaves his latest groans. Sad goes the swain,
Unhooks the steer that mourns his fellow's fate,
And in mid labour leaves the plough-gear fast.
Nor tall wood's shadow, nor soft sward may stir
That heart's emotion, nor rock-channelled flood,
More pure than amber speeding to the plain:
But see! his flanks fail under him, his eyes
Are dulled with deadly torpor, and his neck
Sinks to the earth with drooping weight. What now
Besteads him toil or service? to have turned
The heavy sod with ploughshare? And yet these
Ne'er knew the Massic wine-god's baneful boon,
Nor twice replenished banquets: but on leaves
They fare, and virgin grasses, and their cups
Are crystal springs and streams with running tired,

Their healthful slumbers never broke by care.
Then only, say they, through that country side
For Juno's rites were cattle far to seek,
And ill-matched buffaloes the chariots drew
To their high fanes. So, painfully with rakes
They grub the soil, aye, with their very nails
Dig in the corn-seeds, and with strainèd neck
O'er the high uplands drag the creaking wains.
No wolf for ambush pries about the pen,
Nor round the flock prowls nightly; pain more sharp
Subdues him: the shy deer and fleet-foot stags
With hounds now wander by the haunts of men.
Vast ocean's offspring, and all tribes that swim,
On the shore's confine the wave washes up,
Like shipwrecked bodies: seals, unwonted there,
Flee to the rivers. Now the viper dies,
For all his den's close winding, and with scales
Erect the astonied water-worms. The air
Brooks not the very birds, that headlong fall,
And leave their life beneath the soaring cloud.
Moreover now nor change of fodder serves,
And subtlest cures but injure; then were foiled
The masters, Chiron sprung from Phillyron,
And Amythaon's son Melampus. See!
From Stygian darkness launched into the light
Comes raging pale Tisiphone; she drives
Disease and fear before her, day by day
Still rearing higher that all-devouring head.
With bleat of flocks and lowings thick resound
Rivers and parchèd banks and sloping heights.
At last in crowds she slaughters them, she chokes
The very stalls with carrion-heaps that rot
In hideous corruption, till men learn
With earth to cover them, in pits to hide.
For e'en the fells are useless; nor the flesh
With water may they purge, or tame with fire,
Nor shear the fleeces even, gnawed through and through
With foul disease, nor touch the putrid webs;
But, had one dared the loathly weeds to try,
Red blisters and an unclean sweat o'erran
His noisome limbs, till, no long tarriance made,
The fiery curse his tainted frame devoured.

# GEORGIC IV

Of air-born honey, gift of heaven, I now
Take up the tale. Upon this theme no less
Look thou, Maecenas, with indulgent eye.
A marvellous display of puny powers,
High-hearted chiefs, a nation's history,
Its traits, its bent, its battles and its clans,
All, each, shall pass before you, while I sing.
Slight though the poet's theme, not slight the praise,
So frown not heaven, and Phoebus hear his call.
    First find your bees a settled sure abode,
Where neither winds can enter (winds blow back
The foragers with food returning home)
Nor sheep and butting kids tread down the flowers,
Nor heifer wandering wide upon the plain
Dash off the dew, and bruise the springing blades.
Let the gay lizard too keep far aloof
His scale-clad body from their honied stalls,
And the bee-eater, and what birds beside,
And Procne smirched with blood upon the breast
From her own murderous hands. For these roam wide
Wasting all substance, or the bees themselves
Strike flying, and in their beaks bear home, to glut
Those savage nestlings with the dainty prey.
But let clear springs and moss-green pools be near,
And through the grass a streamlet hurrying run,
Some palm-tree o'er the porch extend its shade,
Or huge-grown oleaster, that in Spring,
Their own sweet Spring-tide, when the new-made chiefs
Lead forth the young swarms, and, escaped their comb,
The colony comes forth to sport and play,
The neighbouring bank may lure them from the heat,

Or bough befriend with hospitable shade.
O'er the mid-waters, whether swift or still,
Cast willow-branches and big stones enow,
Bridge after bridge, where they may footing find
And spread their wide wings to the summer sun,
If haply Eurus, swooping as they pause,
Have dashed with spray or plunged them in the deep.
And let green cassias and far-scented thymes,
And savory with its heavy-laden breath
Bloom round about, and violet-beds hard by
Sip sweetness from the fertilizing springs.
For the hive's self, or stitched of hollow bark,
Or from tough osier woven, let the doors
Be strait of entrance; for stiff winter's cold
Congeals the honey, and heat resolves and thaws,
To bees alike disastrous; not for naught
So haste they to cement the tiny pores
That pierce their walls, and fill the crevices
With pollen from the flowers, and glean and keep
To this same end the glue, that binds more fast
Than bird-lime or the pitch from Ida's pines.
Oft too in burrowed holes, if fame be true,
They make their cosy subterranean home,
And deeply lodged in hollow rocks are found,
Or in the cavern of an age-hewn tree.
Thou not the less smear round their crannied cribs
With warm smooth mud-coat, and strew leaves above;
But near their home let neither yew-tree grow,
Nor reddening crabs be roasted, and mistrust
Deep marish-ground and mire with noisome smell,
Or where the hollow rocks sonorous ring,
And the word spoken buffets and rebounds.
    What more? When now the golden sun has put
Winter to headlong flight beneath the world,
And oped the doors of heaven with summer ray,
Forthwith they roam the glades and forests o'er,
Rifle the painted flowers, or sip the streams,
Light-hovering on the surface. Hence it is
With some sweet rapture, that we know not of,
Their little ones they foster, hence with skill
Work out new wax or clinging honey mould.
So when the cage-escapèd hosts you see
Float heavenward through the hot clear air, until

You marvel at yon dusky cloud that spreads
And lengthens on the wind, then mark them well;
For then 'tis ever the fresh springs they seek
And bowery shelter: hither must you bring
The savoury sweets I bid, and sprinkle them,
Bruised balsam and the wax-flower's lowly weed,
And wake and shake the tinkling cymbals heard
By the great Mother: on the anointed spots
Themselves will settle, and in wonted wise
Seek of themselves the cradle's inmost depth.
   But if to battle they have hied them forth—
For oft 'twixt king and king with uproar dire
Fierce feud arises, and at once from far
You may discern what passion sways the mob,
And how their hearts are throbbing for the strife;
Hark! the hoarse brazen note that warriors know
Chides on the loiterers, and the ear may catch
A sound that mocks the war-trump's broken blasts;
Then in hot haste they muster, then flash wings,
Sharpen their pointed beaks and knit their thews,
And round the king, even to his royal tent,
Throng rallying, and with shouts defy the foe.
So, when a dry Spring and clear space is given,
Forth from the gates they burst, they clash on high;
A din arises; they are heaped and rolled
Into one mighty mass, and headlong fall,
Not denselier hail through heaven, nor pelting so
Rains from the shaken oak its acorn-shower.
Conspicuous by their wings the chiefs themselves
Press through the heart of battle, and display
A giant's spirit in each pigmy frame,
Steadfast no inch to yield till these or those
The victor's ponderous arm has turned to flight.
Such fiery passions and such fierce assaults
A little sprinkled dust controls and quells.
And now, both leaders from the field recalled,
Who hath the worser seeming, do to death,
Lest royal waste wax burdensome, but let
His better lord it on the empty throne.
One with gold-burnished flakes will shine like fire,
For twofold are their kinds, the nobler he,
Of peerless front and lit with flashing scales;
That other, from neglect and squalor foul,

Drags slow a cumbrous belly. As with kings,
So too with people, diverse is their mould,
Some rough and loathly, as when the wayfarer
Scapes from a whirl of dust, and scorched with heat
Spits forth the dry grit from his parchèd mouth:
The others shine forth and flash with lightning-gleam,
Their backs all blazoned with bright drops of gold
Symmetric: this the likelier breed; from these,
When heaven brings round the season, thou shalt strain
Sweet honey, nor yet so sweet as passing clear,
And mellowing on the tongue the wine-god's fire.

   But when the swarms fly aimlessly abroad,
Disport themselves in heaven and spurn their cells,
Leaving the hive unwarmed, from such vain play
Must you refrain their volatile desires,
Nor hard the task: tear off the monarchs' wings;
While these prove loiterers, none beside will dare
Mount heaven, or pluck the standards from the camp.
Let gardens with the breath of saffron flowers
Allure them, and the lord of Hellespont,
Priapus, wielder of the willow-scythe,
Safe in his keeping hold from birds and thieves.
And let the man to whom such cares are dear
Himself bring thyme and pine-trees from the heights,
And strew them in broad belts about their home;
No hand but his the blistering task should ply,
Plant the young slips, or shed the genial showers.

   And I myself, were I not even now
Furling my sails, and, nigh the journey's end,
Eager to turn my vessel's prow to shore,
Perchance would sing what careful husbandry
Makes the trim garden smile; of Paestum too,
Whose roses bloom and fade and bloom again;
How endives glory in the streams they drink,
And green banks in their parsley, and how the gourd
Twists through the grass and rounds him to paunch;
Nor of Narcissus had my lips been dumb,
That loiterer of the flowers, nor supple-stemmed
Acanthus, with the praise of ivies pale,
And myrtles clinging to the shores they love.
For 'neath the shade of tall Oebalia's towers,
Where dark Galaesus laves the yellowing fields,
An old man once I mind me to have seen—

From Corycus he came—to whom had fallen
Some few poor acres of neglected land,
And they nor fruitful 'neath the plodding steer,
Meet for the grazing herd, nor good for vines.
Yet he, the while his meagre garden-herbs
Among the thorns he planted, and all round
White lilies, vervains, and lean poppy set,
In pride of spirit matched the wealth of kings,
And home returning not till night was late,
With unbought plenty heaped his board on high.
He was the first to cull the rose in spring,
He the ripe fruits in autumn; and ere yet
Winter had ceased in sullen ire to rive
The rocks with frost, and with her icy bit
Curb in the running waters, there was he
Plucking the rathe faint hyacinth, while he chid
Summer's slow footsteps and the lagging West.
Therefore he too with earliest brooding bees
And their full swarms o'erflowed, and first was he
To press the bubbling honey from the comb;
Lime-trees were his, and many a branching pine;
And all the fruits wherewith in early bloom
The orchard-tree had clothed her, in full tale
Hung there, by mellowing autumn perfected.
He too transplanted tall-grown elms a-row,
Time-toughened pear, thorns bursting with the plum
And plane now yielding serviceable shade
For dry lips to drink under: but these things,
Shut off by rigorous limits, I pass by,
And leave for others to sing after me.
    Come, then, I will unfold the natural powers
Great Jove himself upon the bees bestowed,
The boon for which, led by the shrill sweet strains
Of the Curetes and their clashing brass,
They fed the King of heaven in Dicte's cave.
Alone of all things they receive and hold
Community of offspring, and they house
Together in one city, and beneath
The shelter of majestic laws they live;
And they alone fixed home and country know,
And in the summer, warned of coming cold,
Make proof of toil, and for the general store
Hoard up their gathered harvesting. For some

Watch o'er the victualling of the hive, and these
By settled order ply their tasks afield;
And some within the confines of their home
Plant firm the comb's first layer, Narcissus' tear,
And sticky gum oozed from the bark of trees,
Then set the clinging wax to hang therefrom.
Others the while lead forth the full-grown young,
Their country's hope, and others press and pack
The thrice repurèd honey, and stretch their cells
To bursting with the clear-strained nectar sweet.
Some, too, the wardship of the gates befalls,
Who watch in turn for showers and cloudy skies,
Or ease returning labourers of their load,
Or form a band and from their precincts drive
The drones, a lazy herd. How glows the work!
How sweet the honey smells of perfumed thyme
Like the Cyclopes, when in haste they forge
From the slow-yielding ore the thunderbolts,
Some from the bull's-hide bellows in and out
Let the blasts drive, some dip i' the water-trough
The sputtering metal: with the anvil's weight
Groans Etna: they alternately in time
With giant strength uplift their sinewy arms,
Or twist the iron with the forceps' grip—
Not otherwise, to measure small with great,
The love of getting planted in their breasts
Goads on the bees, that haunt old Cecrops' heights,
Each in his sphere to labour. The old have charge
To keep the town, and build the wallèd combs,
And mould the cunning chambers; but the youth,
Their tired legs packed with thyme, come labouring home
Belated, for afar they range to feed
On arbutes and the grey-green willow-leaves,
And cassia and the crocus blushing red,
Glue-yielding limes, and hyacinths dusky-eyed.
One hour for rest have all, and one for toil:
With dawn they hurry from the gates—no room
For loiterers there: and once again, when even
Now bids them quit their pasturing on the plain,
Then homeward make they, then refresh their strength:
A hum arises: hark! they buzz and buzz
About the doors and threshold; till at length
Safe laid to rest they hush them for the night,

And welcome slumber laps their weary limbs.
But from the homestead not too far they fare,
When showers hang like to fall, nor, east winds nigh,
Confide in heaven, but 'neath the city walls
Safe-circling fetch them water, or essay
Brief out-goings, and oft weigh-up tiny stones,
As light craft ballast in the tossing tide,
Wherewith they poise them through the cloudy vast.
This law of life, too, by the bees obeyed,
Will move thy wonder, that nor sex with sex
Yoke they in marriage, nor yield their limbs to love,
Nor know the pangs of labour, but alone
From leaves and honied herbs, the mothers, each,
Gather their offspring in their mouths, alone
Supply new kings and pigmy commonwealth,
And their old court and waxen realm repair.
Oft, too, while wandering, against jaggèd stones
Their wings they fray, and 'neath the burden yield
Their liberal lives: so deep their love of flowers,
So glorious deem they honey's proud acquist.
Therefore, though each a life of narrow span,
Ne'er stretched to summers more than seven, befalls,
Yet deathless doth the race endure, and still
Perennial stands the fortune of their line,
From grandsire unto grandsire backward told.
Moreover, not Aegyptus, nor the realm
Of boundless Lydia, no, nor Parthia's hordes,
Nor Median Hydaspes, to their king
Do such obeisance: lives the king unscathed,
One will inspires the million: is he dead,
Snapt is the bond of fealty; they themselves
Ravage their toil-wrought honey, and rend amain
Their own comb's waxen trellis. He is the lord
Of all their labour; him with awful eye
They reverence, and with murmuring throngs surround,
In crowds attend, oft shoulder him on high,
Or with their bodies shield him in the fight,
And seek through showering wounds a glorious death.
  Led by these tokens, and with such traits to guide,
Some say that unto bees a share is given
Of the Divine Intelligence, and to drink
Pure draughts of ether; for God permeates all—
Earth, and wide ocean, and the vault of heaven—

From whom flocks, herds, men, beasts of every kind,
Draw each at birth the fine essential flame;
Yea, and that all things hence to Him return,
Brought back by dissolution, nor can death
Find place: but, each into his starry rank,
Alive they soar, and mount the heights of heaven.

If now their narrow home thou wouldst unseal,
And broach the treasures of the honey-house,
With draught of water first foment thy lips,
And spread before thee fumes of trailing smoke.
Twice is the teeming produce gathered in,
Twofold their time of harvest year by year,
Once when Taygete the Pleiad uplifts
Her comely forehead for the earth to see,
With foot of scorn spurning the ocean-streams,
Once when in gloom she flies the watery Fish,
And dips from heaven into the wintry wave.
Unbounded then their wrath; if hurt, they breathe
Venom into their bite, cleave to the veins
And let the sting lie buried, and leave their lives
Behind them in the wound. But if you dread
Too rigorous a winter, and would fain
Temper the coming time, and their bruised hearts
And broken estate to pity move thy soul,
Yet who would fear to fumigate with thyme,
Or cut the empty wax away? for oft
Into their comb the newt has gnawed unseen,
And the light-loathing beetles crammed their bed,
And he that sits at others' board to feast,
The do-naught drone; or 'gainst the unequal foe
Swoops the fierce hornet, or the moth's fell tribe;
Or spider, victim of Minerva's spite,
Athwart the doorway hangs her swaying net.
The more impoverished they, the keenlier all
To mend the fallen fortunes of their race
Will nerve them, fill the cells up, tier on tier,
And weave their granaries from the rifled flowers.

Now, seeing that life doth even to bee-folk bring
Our human chances, if in dire disease
Their bodies' strength should languish—which anon
By no uncertain tokens may be told—
Forthwith the sick change hue; grim leanness mars
Their visage; then from out the cells they bear

Forms reft of light, and lead the mournful pomp;
Or foot to foot about the porch they hang,
Or within closed doors loiter, listless all
From famine, and benumbed with shrivelling cold.
Then is a deep note heard, a long-drawn hum,
As when the chill South through the forests sighs,
As when the troubled ocean hoarsely booms
With back-swung billow, as ravening tide of fire
Surges, shut fast within the furnace-walls.
Then do I bid burn scented galbanum,
And, honey-streams through reeden troughs instilled,
Challenge and cheer their flagging appetite
To taste the well-known food; and it shall boot
To mix therewith the savour bruised from gall,
And rose-leaves dried, or must to thickness boiled
By a fierce fire, or juice of raisin-grapes
From Psithian vine, and with its bitter smell
Centaury, and the famed Cecropian thyme.
There is a meadow-flower by country folk
Hight star-wort; 'tis a plant not far to seek;
For from one sod an ample growth it rears,
Itself all golden, but girt with plenteous leaves,
Where glory of purple shines through violet gloom.
With chaplets woven hereof full oft are decked
Heaven's altars: harsh its taste upon the tongue;
Shepherds in vales smooth-shorn of nibbling flocks
By Mella's winding waters gather it.
The roots of this, well seethed in fragrant wine,
Set in brimmed baskets at their doors for food.
    But if one's whole stock fail him at a stroke,
Nor hath he whence to breed the race anew,
'Tis time the wondrous secret to disclose
Taught by the swain of Arcady, even how
The blood of slaughtered bullocks oft has borne
Bees from corruption. I will trace me back
To its prime source the story's tangled thread,
And thence unravel. For where thy happy folk,
Canopus, city of Pellaean fame,
Dwell by the Nile's lagoon-like overflow,
And high o'er furrows they have called their own
Skim in their painted wherries; where, hard by,
The quivered Persian presses, and that flood
Which from the swart-skinned Aethiop bears him down,

Swift-parted into sevenfold branching mouths
With black mud fattens and makes Aegypt green,
That whole domain its welfare's hope secure
Rests on this art alone. And first is chosen
A strait recess, cramped closer to this end,
Which next with narrow roof of tiles atop
'Twixt prisoning walls they pinch, and add hereto
From the four winds four slanting window-slits.
Then seek they from the herd a steer, whose horns
With two years' growth are curling, and stop fast,
Plunge madly as he may, the panting mouth
And nostrils twain, and done with blows to death,
Batter his flesh to pulp i' the hide yet whole,
And shut the doors, and leave him there to lie.
But 'neath his ribs they scatter broken boughs,
With thyme and fresh-pulled cassias: this is done
When first the west winds bid the waters flow,
Ere flush the meadows with new tints, and ere
The twittering swallow buildeth from the beams.
Meanwhile the juice within his softened bones
Heats and ferments, and things of wondrous birth,
Footless at first, anon with feet and wings,
Swarm there and buzz, a marvel to behold;
And more and more the fleeting breeze they take,
Till, like a shower that pours from summer-clouds,
Forth burst they, or like shafts from quivering string
When Parthia's flying hosts provoke the fray.

  Say what was he, what God, that fashioned forth
This art for us, O Muses? of man's skill
Whence came the new adventure? From thy vale,
Peneian Tempe, turning, bee-bereft,
So runs the tale, by famine and disease,
Mournful the shepherd Aristaeus stood
Fast by the haunted river-head, and thus
With many a plaint to her that bare him cried:
"Mother, Cyrene, mother, who hast thy home
Beneath this whirling flood, if he thou sayest,
Apollo, lord of Thymbra, be my sire,
Sprung from the Gods' high line, why barest thou me
With fortune's ban for birthright? Where is now
Thy love to me-ward banished from thy breast?
O! wherefore didst thou bid me hope for heaven?
Lo! even the crown of this poor mortal life,

Which all my skilful care by field and fold,
No art neglected, scarce had fashioned forth,
Even this falls from me, yet thou call'st me son.
Nay, then, arise! With thine own hands pluck up
My fruit-plantations: on the homestead fling
Pitiless fire; make havoc of my crops;
Burn the young plants, and wield the stubborn axe
Against my vines, if there hath taken thee
Such loathing of my greatness." But that cry,
Even from her chamber in the river-deeps,
His mother heard: around her spun the nymphs
Milesian wool stained through with hyaline dye,
Drymo, Xantho, Ligea, Phyllodoce,
Their glossy locks o'er snowy shoulders shed,
Cydippe and Lycorias yellow-haired,
A maiden one, one newly learned even then
To bear Lucina's birth-pang. Clio, too,
And Beroe, sisters, ocean-children both,
Both zoned with gold and girt with dappled fell,
Ephyre and Opis, and from Asian meads
Deiopea, and, bow at length laid by,
Fleet-footed Arethusa. But in their midst
Fair Clymene was telling o'er the tale
Of Vulcan's idle vigilance and the stealth
Of Mars' sweet rapine, and from Chaos old
Counted the jostling love-joys of the Gods.
Charmed by whose lay, the while their woolly tasks
With spindles down they drew, yet once again
Smote on his mother's ears the mournful plaint
Of Aristaeus; on their glassy thrones
Amazement held them all; but Arethuse
Before the rest put forth her auburn head,
Peering above the wave-top, and from far
Exclaimed, "Cyrene, sister. not for naught
Scared by a groan so deep, behold! 'tis he,
Even Aristaeus, thy heart's fondest care,
Here by the brink of the Peneian sire
Stands woebegone and weeping, and by name
Cries out upon thee for thy cruelty."
To whom, strange terror knocking at her heart,
"Bring, bring him to our sight," the mother cried;
"His feet may tread the threshold even of Gods."
So saying, she bids the flood yawn wide and yield

A pathway for his footsteps; but the wave
Arched mountain-wise closed round him, and within
Its mighty bosom welcomed, and let speed
To the deep river-bed. And now, with eyes
Of wonder gazing on his mother's hall
And watery kingdom and cave-prisoned pools
And echoing groves, he went, and, stunned by that
Stupendous whirl of waters, separate saw
All streams beneath the mighty earth that glide,
Phasis and Lycus, and that fountain-head
Whence first the deep Enipeus leaps to light,
Whence father Tiber, and whence Anio's flood,
And Hypanis that roars amid his rocks,
And Mysian Caicus, and, bull-browed
'Twixt either gilded horn, Eridanus,
Than whom none other through the laughing plains
More furious pours into the purple sea.
Soon as the chamber's hanging roof of stone
Was gained, and now Cyrene from her son
Had heard his idle weeping, in due course
Clear water for his hands the sisters bring,
With napkins of shorn pile, while others heap
The board with dainties, and set on afresh
The brimming goblets; with Panchaian fires
Upleap the altars; then the mother spake,
"Take beakers of Maeonian wine," she said,
"Pour we to Ocean." Ocean, sire of all,
She worships, and the sister-nymphs who guard
The hundred forests and the hundred streams;
Thrice Vesta's fire with nectar clear she dashed,
Thrice to the roof-top shot the flame and shone:
Armed with which omen she essayed to speak:
"In Neptune's gulf Carpathian dwells a seer,
Caerulean Proteus, he who metes the main
With fish-drawn chariot of two-footed steeds;
Now visits he his native home once more,
Pallene and the Emathian ports; to him
We nymphs do reverence, ay, and Nereus old;
For all things knows the seer, both those which are
And have been, or which time hath yet to bring;
So willed it Neptune, whose portentous flocks,
And loathly sea-calves 'neath the surge he feeds.
Him first, my son, behoves thee seize and bind,

That he may all the cause of sickness show,
And grant a prosperous end. For save by force
No rede will he vouchsafe, nor shalt thou bend
His soul by praying; whom once made captive, ply
With rigorous force and fetters; against these
His wiles will break and spend themselves in vain.
I, when the sun has lit his noontide fires,
When the blades thirst, and cattle love the shade,
Myself will guide thee to the old man's haunt,
Whither he hies him weary from the waves,
That thou mayst safelier steal upon his sleep.
But when thou hast gripped him fast with hand and gyve,
Then divers forms and bestial semblances
Shall mock thy grasp; for sudden he will change
To bristly boar, fell tigress, dragon scaled,
And tawny-tufted lioness, or send forth
A crackling sound of fire, and so shake off
The fetters, or in showery drops anon
Dissolve and vanish. But the more he shifts
His endless transformations, thou, my son,
More straitlier clench the clinging bands, until
His body's shape return to that thou sawest,
When with closed eyelids first he sank to sleep."
    So saying, an odour of ambrosial dew
She sheds around, and all his frame therewith
Steeps throughly; forth from his trim-combèd locks
Breathed effluence sweet, and a lithe vigour leapt
Into his limbs. There is a cavern vast
Scooped in the mountain-side, where wave on wave
By the wind's stress is driven, and breaks far up
Its inmost creeks—safe anchorage from of old
For tempest-taken mariners: therewithin,
Behind a rock's huge barrier, Proteus hides.
Here in close covert out of the sun's eye
The youth she places, and herself the while
Swathed in a shadowy mist stands far aloof.
And now the ravening dog-star that burns up
The thirsty Indians blazed in heaven; his course
The fiery sun had half devoured: the blades
Were parched, and the void streams with droughty jaws
Baked to their mud-beds by the scorching ray,
When Proteus seeking his accustomed cave
Strode from the billows: round him frolicking

The watery folk that people the waste sea
Sprinkled the bitter brine-dew far and wide.
Along the shore in scattered groups to feed
The sea-calves stretch them: while the seer himself,
Like herdsman on the hills when evening bids
The steers from pasture to their stall repair,
And the lambs' bleating whets the listening wolves,
Sits midmost on the rock and tells his tale.
But Aristaeus, the foe within his clutch,
Scarce suffering him compose his agèd limbs,
With a great cry leapt on him, and ere he rose
Forestalled him with the fetters; he nathless,
All unforgetful of his ancient craft,
Transforms himself to every wondrous thing,
Fire and a fearful beast, and flowing stream.
But when no trickery found a path for flight,
Baffled at length, to his own shape returned,
With human lips he spake, "Who bade thee, then,
So reckless in youth's hardihood, affront
Our portals? or what wouldst thou hence?"—But he,
"Proteus, thou knowest, of thine own heart thou knowest;
For thee there is no cheating, but cease thou
To practise upon me: at heaven's behest
I for my fainting fortunes hither come
An oracle to ask thee." There he ceased.
Whereat the seer, by stubborn force constrained,
Shot forth the grey light of his gleaming eyes
Upon him, and with fiercely gnashing teeth
Unlocks his lips to spell the fates of heaven:
  "Doubt not 'tis wrath divine that plagues thee thus,
Nor light the debt thou payest; 'tis Orpheus' self,
Orpheus unhappy by no fault of his,
So fates prevent not, fans thy penal fires,
Yet madly raging for his ravished bride.
She in her haste to shun thy hot pursuit
Along the stream, saw not the coming death,
Where at her feet kept ward upon the bank
In the tall grass a monstrous water-snake.
But with their cries the Dryad-band her peers
Filled up the mountains to their proudest peaks:
Wailed for her fate the heights of Rhodope,
And tall Pangaea, and, beloved of Mars;
The land that bowed to Rhesus, Thrace no less

With Hebrus' stream; and Orithyia wept,
Daughter of Acte old. But Orpheus' self,
Soothing his love-pain with the hollow shell,
Thee his sweet wife on the lone shore alone,
Thee when day dawned and when it died he sang.
Nay to the jaws of Taenarus too he came,
Of Dis the infernal palace, and the grove
Grim with a horror of great darkness—came,
Entered, and faced the Manes and the King
Of terrors, the stone heart no prayer can tame.
Then from the deepest deeps of Erebus,
Wrung by his minstrelsy, the hollow shades
Came trooping, ghostly semblances of forms
Lost to the light, as birds by myriads hie
To greenwood boughs for cover, when twilight-hour
Or storms of winter chase them from the hills;
Matrons and men, and great heroic frames
Done with life's service, boys, unwedded girls,
Youths placed on pyre before their fathers' eyes.
Round them, with black slime choked and hideous weed,
Cocytus winds; there lies the unlovely swamp
Of dull dead water, and, to pen them fast,
Styx with her ninefold barrier poured between.
Nay, even the deep Tartarean Halls of death
Stood lost in wonderment, and the Eumenides,
Their brows with livid locks of serpents twined;
Even Cerberus held his triple jaws agape,
And, the wind hushed, Ixion's wheel stood still.
And now with homeward footstep he had passed
All perils scathless, and, at length restored,
Eurydice to realms of upper air
Had well-nigh won, behind him following—
So Proserpine had ruled it—when his heart
A sudden mad desire surprised and seized—
Meet fault to be forgiven, might Hell forgive.
For at the very threshold of the day,
Heedless, alas! and vanquished of resolve,
He stopped, turned, looked upon Eurydice
His own once more. But even with the look,
Poured out was all his labour, broken the bond
Of that fell tyrant, and a crash was heard
Three times like thunder in the meres of hell.
'Orpheus! what ruin hath thy frenzy wrought

On me, alas! and thee? Lo! once again
The unpitying fates recall me, and dark sleep
Closes my swimming eyes. And now farewell:
Girt with enormous night I am borne away,
Outstretching toward thee, thine, alas! no more,
These helpless hands.' She spake, and suddenly,
Like smoke dissolving into empty air,
Passed and was sundered from his sight; nor him
Clutching vain shadows, yearning sore to speak,
Thenceforth beheld she, nor no second time
Hell's boatman brooks he pass the watery bar.
What should he do? fly whither, twice bereaved?
Move with what tears the Manes, with what voice
The Powers of darkness? She indeed even now
Death-cold was floating on the Stygian barge!
For seven whole months unceasingly, men say,
Beneath a skyey crag, by thy lone wave,
Strymon, he wept, and in the caverns chill
Unrolled his story, melting tigers' hearts,
And leading with his lay the oaks along.
As in the poplar-shade a nightingale
Mourns her lost young, which some relentless swain,
Spying, from the nest has torn unfledged, but she
Wails the long night, and perched upon a spray
With sad insistence pipes her dolorous strain,
Till all the region with her wrongs o'erflows.
No love, no new desire, constrained his soul:
By snow-bound Tanais and the icy north,
Far steppes to frost Rhipaean for ever wed,
Alone he wandered, lost Eurydice
Lamenting, and the gifts of Dis ungiven.
Scorned by which tribute the Ciconian dames,
Amid their awful Bacchanalian rites
And midnight revellings, tore him limb from limb,
And strewed his fragments over the wide fields.
Then too, even then, what time the Hebrus stream,
Œagrian Hebrus, down mid-current rolled,
Rent from the marble neck, his drifting head,
The death-chilled tongue found yet a voice to cry
'Eurydice! ah! poor Eurydice!'
With parting breath he called her, and the banks
From the broad stream caught up 'Eurydice!'"
    So Proteus ending plunged into the deep,

And, where he plunged, beneath the eddying whirl
Churned into foam the water, and was gone;
But not Cyrene, who unquestioned thus
Bespake the trembling listener: "Nay, my son,
From that sad bosom thou mayst banish care:
Hence came that plague of sickness, hence the nymphs,
With whom in the tall woods the dance she wove,
Wrought on thy bees, alas! this deadly bane.
Bend thou before the Dell-nymphs, gracious powers:
Bring gifts, and sue for pardon: they will grant
Peace to thine asking, and an end of wrath.
But how to approach them will I first unfold—
Four chosen bulls of peerless form and bulk,
That browse to-day the green Lycaean heights,
Pick from thy herds, as many kine to match,
Whose necks the yoke pressed never: then for these
Build up four altars by the lofty fanes,
And from their throats let gush the victims' blood,
And in the greenwood leave their bodies lone.
Then, when the ninth dawn hath displayed its beams,
To Orpheus shalt thou send his funeral dues,
Poppies of Lethe, and let slay a sheep
Coal-black, then seek the grove again, and soon
For pardon found adore Eurydice
With a slain calf for victim."
                        No delay:
The self-same hour he hies him forth to do
His mother's bidding: to the shrine he came,
The appointed altars reared, and thither led
Four chosen bulls of peerless form and bulk,
With kine to match, that never yoke had known;
Then, when the ninth dawn had led in the day,
To Orpheus sent his funeral dues, and sought
The grove once more. But sudden, strange to tell!
A portent they espy: through the oxen's flesh,
Waxed soft in dissolution, hark! there hum
Bees from the belly; the rent ribs overboil!
In endless clouds they spread them, till at last
On yon tree-top together fused they cling,
And drop their cluster from the bending boughs.
  So sang I of the tilth of furrowed fields,
Of flocks and trees, while Caesar's majesty
Launched forth the levin-bolts of war by deep

Euphrates, and bare rule o'er willing folk
Though vanquished, and essayed the heights of heaven.
I Virgil then, of sweet Parthenope
The nursling, wooed the flowery walks of peace
Inglorious, who erst trilled for shepherd-wights
The wanton ditty, and sang in saucy youth
Thee, Tityrus, 'neath the spreading beech tree's shade.